SOMETIMES I CRY

CRY

LINDA DOMINIQUE GROSVENOR

Published By
Milligan Books

Cover Design By
Chris Ebuehi – Graphic Options

Formatted by
Black Butterfly Press

ISBN 1-881524-38-8

Dedication

This book is dedicated to the fact that life is an ongoing learning process.

Acknowledgements:

I would like to thank my King Jesus for anointing my hands, and bringing forth fruit that will help heal those who are suffering through the situations that the characters in this book struggle with. I thank Him for giving me insight into His Word and approving my finished product. You have given your life Jesus, all I can offer is mine.

I would like to thank my mom for the faith she has in me, and the way she questions and helps me tie up the loose ends in everything. Remember all things work together for good. I pray that we all find peace by allowing ourselves to be made over in His image.

I would like to thank Victoria Christopher Murray who helped me calm my fears and the anxiety of publishing my first piece, and literally brought me out of the literary closet. I thank her for all the long drawn out e-mails she responded to and the never-ending questions she answered while I was "decorating." You have offered your service in love and without question. You are a blessing. I have never met anyone as self-less as you!

To my sisters (Judie, Janet), brother (Melvin), son (Jamel), niece (Akila), nephews (Melvin Jr. and Jalen), and long time friends and family, I just want to thank you all for your patience in anticipating this book that I have been saying that I was writing for years. Finally here it is. Rejoice with me. God is good!

I would love to thank Melvin R. D. Shockley for making time in his busy schedule to read my manuscript, and for being a constant support. You were full of questions and I thank you for liking my characters and the outcome before they were

I want to thank you Timmothy B. McCann for keeping me laughing. It means so much in the day to day, you can't begin to imagine. You are real and down to earth. Thank you for convincing me that I can be the "queen" of New York!

To all my girls at Nyack, you have been an inspiration from the beginning. Thank you for being excited for me from the start. I knew all along that with God all things were possible, I just thank you all for the reassurance. Keep praying, the war is not over. There is a book in all of you, too!

Dr. Rosie Milligan, I thank you for believing in a girl from New York who had a story that she was anxious to tell. I am grateful for you taking me under your wing and the chance you gave me to share this story with the world.

To the man who inspired this book. Life is indeed a learning experience and we all learn from mistakes we make. Marriage is meant to be a lifetime commitment. We should go into it realizing that. We should never allow or be persuaded into marriage as a cover-up to sin. We must seek God in all things, most of all, our life mate! Our decisions can and do affect the rest of our lives.

I'd also like to thank, Abundant Life Tabernacle, Cynthia Givens (God is good like that!), Shunda Blocker, Edwin Pasco, Tia Shabazz and the African American Online Writer's Guild, Dr. Edwin McAllister & The Little Brown Handbook, Wayne Pinkney, Tim Jones, Veda Brown and Net Noir, Joel Domingue, Liliane Louis, Dominique Louis, The Poetry Society of America, The Family Violence Prevention Fund, and all those who somehow or another nurtured or supported my poetry and writing ability. If I forgot anyone, I'm sorry, God didn't.

Chapter One

I have never been more anxious in my entire life than I am right now. I'm sitting at my desk with an hour or more to kill and a list of things that must get done before 9:00 P.M. Paperwork is everywhere, my half-eaten lunch is still in the styrofoam, and I have coffee stains all over my to-do list.

"Calm down, Aaliyah," I told myself. I had to pick up my favorite navy **Versace** suit from the cleaners for Monday's meeting, get my diamond studs out of the safety deposit box, go to the dentist to have the wires on my teeth tightened, which I hated, go home, shower and change, breathe and relax, then meet Mark 'at **B. Smith's** on 8th Avenue. That's Mark's "We need to talk" place.

I'm really not in the mood for Mark's drama tonight. I refuse to sit and figure out if he loves me or he loves me not. I've been there and hated it. Tonight I'm turning the tables. I've created a scenario of my own. I plan on making a love connection. One minute he makes it all too clear that we are nothing more than friends, and then in the same breath he's inching up on me as soon as someone else shows a little interest.

"You know I love you, Lea," he says matter-of-factly. He's just like a child that doesn't want a toy until another kid picks it up and starts playing with it. Any other time the "toy" is being kicked around the floor and walked on, and he could care less.

He says I'm pushy, I say he's confused, and in the end I know I'm right. He has an abnormal personality, and he sends mixed signals. One day he wants me to bear his children and the next day he's telling me how he's gotten hurt in the past and isn't sure if it's the right time for us.

"What does that mean?" If I left it up to him it would never be the right time for us.

My friends all think he's gay, although I don't think so. "That's not even it" I tell them. His problem is that he is scared to death of love. The "c" word. Commitment! He's terrified. Who would think that a mere ten-letter word could weaken a man to the point that he's confused and incoherent? He thinks that the minute we are officially deemed a couple that we have to move in to gether or get married. He also assumes that by allowing me to believe that he's not in love with me that I (being totally and completely in love with him) will stick around hoping, wishing, and futilely trying to change him.

He also assumes that if he does ever reveal his deepest and innermost feelings to me that he'd get an adverse reaction, like I'd leave or something. In a nutshell, he wants to have his cake and eat it too. Men. What can you do? You can't live without them. I mean, you can try but there will always be a void. Life wasn't meant to live alone.

God created man and woman for more than just procreation, and it had a lot more to do with preventing loneliness than we'd like to think. Although, if you got the wrong man you could still end up feeling lonelier than you

2

would if you were by yourself. Without someone to love though, something would always be missing, and without love you will never fully become and experience what you are to know and be in life, unless of course, you were called to celibacy. But that's another story.

The fact is that without a significant other, who would you share your life, hopes and dreams with? Without someone special, there would always be a void. An empty space that you put other things in, trying to make them fit, and in the end you'll discover that there's still an empty space. "I don't need a man to validate me as a woman!" Women who say that are bitter and doomed to be spinsters. Find that same woman the right man and she'll mutate into something reminiscent of a fourteen-year-old schoolgirl. Hypocrites!

Mark and I have been estranged for about a month. We had a major disagreement, and instead of letting bygones be bygones he wanted to play the "who can hold out on calling the longest" game. Needless to say, I won.

"Women have more control than men do," I told him. I laughed, he didn't. He always wore his machismo like a suit of armor. Full of pride is what he is. I did miss him though. I missed the way he hinted and I had to guess what he was insinuating. He was never straight forward or to the point. Far be it from him to be obvious. It was always a game with him from day one.

It's a strange sort of relationship we have because Mark and I usually chat daily and inquire about each other's day. We get along so well and we have so much in common that it's scary. We agree on almost everything, we have the same weird taste in music, we both love Italian, we love to laugh and we flirt endlessly with each other. Flirting. It's an art that I've mastered to the point that I can teach it or give a seminar about it at *The New School* or the *Learning Annex*.

That's what makes the situation so awkward. We are naturally drawn to each other, it's obvious. He's fighting it, I'm not. I'm ready to take it to the next level and he's afraid that if we do we might lose everything. But tonight, I'm in the convincing business. I have a plan. I've been honest, I've hinted, I've been mysterious, I've lied, and it didn't work. I tried to make him jealous, and that didn't work either. I think I've played fair long enough, now it's time to pull out the heavy artillery. The art of seduction.

He wants to get together tonight to talk? Well, I'll give him something that he'll be talking about for the rest of his life. When he arrives I'll be wearing my long black crepe form-fitting dress from *Byblos*, my diamond earrings, my black stacked heel strappy patent leather sandals and more than a little sienna lip color - courtesy of *Ultima II*. Matte was still in, I didn't care what the woman at the drug store said. She was only trying to get me to buy the new lipstick that they were selling. I was on to her.

I read in an old issue of *Cosmopolitan* that citrus scents triggered childhood memories in men, and I definitely want to reach the child in him tonight. I want to make him lose control. So, *Calyx* is my fragrance of choice. Besides it's my favorite. Some women like my sister Nicky don't know what a good fragrance is. She was still wearing *Giorgio* and *Red Door*. I tried teaching her that the lighter scents were for spring and summer, and the heavier not-so-fruity ones were for winter and fall. She didn't get it, she never did.

Citrus. I could never get tired of this fragrance, I'll only stop wearing it when they stop making it, which I hope was never. I had to create a mood. I had to have him in the palm of my hand. So it was time for my lacy underthings. Did I forget to mention the seductive quality of the *Victoria's Secret* pewter French lace and silk bra set, from the Christmas '96 fantasy issue, that I've been saving for a

4

special occasion? It doesn't get more special than this. Victoria is what I'll be wearing tonight underneath all of the glitz and glamour. It cost enough. Not as much as the diamond miracle bra, but it cost. Not that I plan on wearing any of this for long, because after the drinks and dinner, the second he crosses the threshold of my apartment, the seduction is on and "***BOOM***" he's mine!

My hair will fall flawlessly into place around my face and shoulders, and I'll be a work of art. Literally. I've worked so hard at making my body look this good that I don't think that it would be considered vain to toot my own horn a little bit. An hour every other day and two hours on Saturday in the gym, milk isn't the only thing that does this body good.

And last but not least my fabulous ensemble will be accented with a gorgeous silver and gold ***Fendi*** watch that he got me for Christmas last year. I don't mean to be a namedropper, but if you've got it flaunt it. Besides I don't have any other outlet. I stopped writing in my journal last year after I spent about fourteen weekends in a row watching ***Unsolved Mysteries*** and ***Mad TV***.

Rule number one when on a date is that it is mandatory that you have a conversation piece, and the watch is just that. That way, if the conversation falls into a lull, I can bring up the watch and reminisce a bit. I remember it like it was yesterday, we were just Christmas shopping for a breadmaker for his mother last year when I saw the watch in ***Bloomingdale's*** and had to have it. I whined and laid it on pretty thick and he offered to pay for half of it as my Christmas slash birthday present. Even though it sort of shocked me because I know how "tight" he is with money. He didn't actually give in without a fight though. But then again if I whine and pout long enough I can get just about anything out of him, that's how I know he cares.

5

He implies that he doesn't care as much as I think he does, not in "*that*" way he always says, but actions speak louder than words. He said that I read too much into things. A four-hundred and ninety-five dollar watch? A definite conversation piece, and a lot to read into. Let him tell it, he'll probably say that he got carried away with good will and Christmas cheer and all that sort of stuff, or that he was experiencing a moment of temporary insanity. But I pray that it is just the first of many steps in an obvious gesture of love.

Okay, okay, back to the plan. His favorite color is black so it's only "apropo" that I clad myself in a one-size-too-small black dress. It has to be love. I skipped lunch all week just to fit into this dress. When I think of all the cute things that we do for each other I wonder why he is still denying his feelings. He has a cute little habit of leaving songs on my answering machine, or at least conveniently letting them play in the background. I like it though. Sometimes he plays the entire song and sometimes just the "I wanna be with you forever" part. He says that it doesn't mean anything. "They're just words," he says. Denial is a wonderful sedative.

I think back to Christmas Eve at my place when he stopped by spur of the moment. I didn't even have time to freshen up. I was sitting around in my pajamas with hair pins and doggie slippers. He was lonely or in love, although it doesn't really matter now which. We nearly went all the way. I'm hoping for a repeat performance with a more satisfying outcome.

My sister Nicky is the only one who lives in the same town as me and we usually spend Christmas eve together. But last year she had a date. We usually three-way call Todd and his family and Moma and Cheyenne and then they usually hook up Rhonda. Well, Cheyenne usually has

6

to do it because Moma says she just can't get the hang of this modern technology stuff.

Rhonda is the oldest; she lives in Atlanta with her husband Gene and tries to cope with infidelity and boredom. She plays housewife and Gene plays doctor, with other women. Such a mockery of love. Cheyenne is two years younger than I am and she and Moma have a condo in Port St. Lucie, Florida. Moma retired in 1991 and hightailed it to Florida, she couldn't take another New York City winter. Cheyenne sells life insurance, although she was a business major in college. Todd is two years older than me and as ignorant as a rock. He lives in California with his girlfriend of four years Lisa who is working on baby number four. She gets welfare and he eats up all the food stamps when he should have a job or at least be looking day and night for one.

He's always calling me, talking about "what's up, Sis." He only calls when he wants something and the only thing he always wants is to borrow money. He has no real job, unless you call using their raggedy car as a cab to earn a few extra bucks to buy a "*forty*" a job. I call them dumb and dumber. If she has any more kids she can just start giving them numbers instead of names. I mean people don't have babies like that anymore. Do they? Especially not poor people. But he's content with watching the Knicks lose, and the Jets and Giants fumble.

Lisa's goal in life is to snag the brass ring but if baby number four hasn't done it, it won't get done. I guess we really aren't the Brady bunch. But then Moma never let us watch that show anyway. She said we couldn't relate or identify to them, and how right she was. They were white, lived in suburbia and solved every problem they ever had within the half-hour and with a smile to top it off. We on the other hand were nothing more than an accumulation of mishaps.

Mark had no family except his mother and his estranged delusional father. Mark's mom has been ill for years. I don't know if it's something serious but I know she has something that he doesn't care to mention. She raised her family to be secretive and that probably explains a lot about why Mark can't express himself. His father on the other hand left his mother when he was twelve-years old and now his father has a different little "*trick*" every other month.

I think it's a beyond mid-life crisis thing with his father, since he has to be at least nearing sixty-years old. Mark really doesn't care to talk about his father either, so I don't ask. And for the past two years Mark's been my Christmas Eve companion. I like nice things, Mark knows that. So, I thanked him for the Fendi watch over eggnog and "*It's a Wonderful Life.*" *Babyface* was singing something in the background. The lights chased themselves around my tree and I had to be two clouds from heaven. I think my gratitude overwhelmed him a bit. I kissed him and I'm more than sure he was kissing me back.

It must have been the rum in the eggnog. I imagined that he was my brave knight and that I was Rapunzel being rescued from the tower that my evil step-monster locked me away in. He began to look at me in ways he never had before. His eyes seemed to tell me things his heart denied. He soaked in the little that could be revealed by my pajamas and wore an expression bordering on confession. But the next day he called me and we talked almost as if nothing had happened. He never mentioned the incident or the display of affection that we both shared. That's denial.

He wasn't alone though; I've been in denial too. So much so that I join in with my friends, telling them how good the sex was last night and how he made me have orgasms so magnificent that I saw rainbows. But deep down I was embarrassed to tell them that the reason why so

8

many of my relationships fell apart was really because the men I dated were impressed that I was a virgin, but they weren't too impressed with the fact that I wasn't giving in or giving it up.

Sasha doesn't seem to buy it though; it's like she can see right through me. She always gives me this look like she knows that the only hot thing that Mark and I share is my barbecue chicken that he likes so much. It's not that I don't want to have sex or make love to someone I like. I make it my business to know a lot of guys and mingle, but I want Mark. I go to gallery openings and book signings and meet men who are writers, poets, bankers, teachers and even police officers; it's just that I want to make love with someone that I adore. Someone who loves me, flaws and all. Someone who's going to be around after the cherry is gone. I guess I'm saving myself for Mark. But, he acts like he doesn't even know it.

I say it over and over again, but he thinks everything is a joke. I mean he knows I want to be with him but he doesn't know that tonight he will be the first. He knows all about the men in my life. The good, the bad, the ugly, the impostors and the thieves. I can tell him anything, and I have.

There was this one guy Jerry that I told him about who stole five dollars from my wallet. He followed me home like a puppy, after we ran into each other in the supermart. I had been avoiding him since I found out he was a bum. And while I was in the kitchen preparing a meal to feed the near-homeless-fool he was shuffling through my wallet, talking about he was looking for matches. In the money compartment? The clown didn't even smoke!

There was no doubt in my mind that he did it. I'm pretty precise when it comes to money. I didn't even ask the fool if he took it because he had to be extremely hard-up to stoop that low to begin with. I just stopped returning his phone calls. Besides he only called when he wanted a free meal or when they turned off his cable, which shouldn't have mattered because I think he only had **Nickelodeon** and The Weather Channel or something like that anyway. I hated thieves. Especially ones who said, "I love you."

So, tonight is it. I'll show Mark that none of the others mattered to me and that they never did. "Lea, you've got guts," I said to myself as I finally made up my mind to do it once and for all. Besides if someone else came along and snatched him up before I had the chance to pour out my heart, I would be crushed. After all he is a catch, and he is also here's-my-credit-card and thank-you-Jesus fine.

A little shy of a carat, I picked out the perfect round diamond at my favorite jeweler. Meir was a handsome Greek guy with chiseled features, and a neatly trimmed mustache. And he was always very very helpful. The ring had quality and impressive clarity.

"You have excellent taste, Lea," Meir complimented.

I had chosen a half-carat diamond set in an 18 karat gold band for Mark. Sasha said that I was crazy to buy my own ring but Josai said "Lea, you go girl."

Josai is all for whatever makes me happy and it's nice to have a friend like that. Sasha is sort of my reality check but sometimes she can be a bit of a dark cloud hovering overhead. See, I know that as "frugal" as Mark is that I'd better invest in something I *really* want for myself, or I might end up with something that leaves little to be desired, like a chip or a cubic zirconia.

I mean it doesn't really matter who buys the ring as long as the marriage license is signed in ink, right? This is the 90's. That's why I came up with this plan, not that he's sneaky but he might think that if I love him, that it shouldn't matter what I'm wearing on my finger. That's a lie. I won't deny that I'm materialistic, but there is no way that I'm going to wave a cubic zirconia at my friends and proudly say, "ooo look what he got me" and that goes double for a chip.

I'm a bit of a romantic, I like nice things and I'd like to think of myself as classy too. That makes me an elegant materialistic romantic. I guess I'm not willing to go the route that some women do. I am not going to need a magnifying glass to see the stone in my engagement ring! I'd rather direct my romantic efforts in the directions of ambiance. Creating a scene, and the mood has to be just right, candles, champagne, music and cookies baking in the oven. I mean I never did go along with some of my friends' ideas of "I hardly know you but, spend the night at my apartment, let's have some hard rough sex, then give me some money, and then I demand you to respect me afterwards." I mean, I want strawberries dipped in chocolate, picnics in the park under the stars with soft music playing in the background, and pillowtalk at 2:00 A.M. They call this ideology the Cinderella syndrome but I call it a possibility. I can and will have it.

I'm sure that romance was not just for people in the movies. I know that normal people experienced that type of cuddling, kissing, cooing and loving kind of romance too. I'm tired of watching love on the silver screen and never making it. I'm also tired of playing the waiting game with Mark. I am a bit demanding, and aggressive, to say the least but he's had six years to make a move. He's had six years to decide. I understand cautious and I even understand hesitation, but fear? Confusion? I won't play this game another year, another month, or another day. This evening it's time to make a final decision. Love him or leave him, and I pray it's not the latter.

Chapter Two

The intercom always startles me out of my event-creating mode.

"Lea, Mr. Emerson wants the designs for the Moore account faxed to the San Fernando office a.s.a.p."

I'm an architect, and a very successful one at that. I work for one of the most prestigious firms in New York City. We have succeeded leaps and bounds ahead of the competition. We create fantasies. Lovenests and hideaways complete with spiral staircases, glass ceilings, atriums and jacuzzis. You had to supply your own significant other though. Everybody seemed to want one, but at our prices, only the upper-class bourgeois could afford the pleasure of hot tubs and sensuous evenings where they gazed at their reflections while making love on marble tiles.

My neighbor Nia lives down the hall from me. She decorates homes for a living. I've referred a few of the firm's clients to her. She's decorated at least ten lavish homes in the Briarcliff area for a whopping $5,000 a pop, and that was just her fee. That didn't include the furnishing and accent pieces. She was building a following. Everyone wanted that nouveau look. Modern furniture, hand-carved one of a kind chairs, a fireplace with white bark logs, and a black and white candid shot hanging over it. Nia didn't care if everyone in the entire world wanted the same thing, she got $5,000 per home.

The girl drove a black Lexus jeep with custom designed genuine zebra-skin seats. She owned her co-op apartment free and clear. She wasn't a shop-a-holic but she liked nice things. She dressed her behind off and she didn't have any kids, so decorating was her life. Everyone called her. Sometimes it seems she was invited to dinner parties just to decorate or to give tips for free. She didn't care because she loved it. Some people liked their jobs, some people hated their jobs, but Nia adored hers. "Dream Homes by Nia" is what her business cards said. Whenever anyone asked who decorated the place or where did you get that vase, that table, or that African carving, Nia would be within earshot and she would come running with business cards in hand. Leaping through the room like music was playing, even though it wasn't.

She just finished decorating my bathroom in a pale lilac with Italian marble countertops and tiles, and sterling silver fixtures. It looked more like somewhere you should pull up a chair and eat instead of a place to strip down to your skivvies to shower. All the guys were after Nia too. She was modelesque. She had so many male admirers that the minute one of them sent her flowers, she'd bring the flowers right over to me before the day was out. It kept my apartment fragrant with fresh cuttings that lasted for about a week or until the next dozen came.

She was dating this guy who was training to become a boxer. He was jealous, she was in love, and they were inseparable, enough said. His name was Freddie. He wasn't too much for socializing but he wanted to be wherever she was, and he made it a point to ask questions whether they were necessary or not. He just showed up most of the time.

Appeared out of nowhere, like he could read her mind or something.

"You better watch out" I'd told her.

"He's harmless," she said.

"Nia, don't believe the hype girl," I said, shaking my head at how unlearned and novel she actually was.

Patricia lived one floor down from me. She wasn't what I would label a white friend; she was just a friend. She was married and had a fourteen-year-old son. She'd been married for about fifteen years. I think she was forty-two. I only prayed that I looked that good at forty-two. She had shiny jet black hair and eyes that turned three different shades of green, depending on her mood. She was beautiful, and of Parisian descent. That probably had something to do with it. European women were flawless, or so it seemed. They never gained a pound and they barely wrinkled.

Her husband Sean had a Lexus dealership in White Plains, he had Nia's jeep customized for her. He was one of only two black men who actually owned a Lexus dealership. Her son Justin was the product of an interracial marriage, which didn't seem to bother him. He was counting the year and two months until he was sixteen-years old and could drive. She dreaded it.

For now Pat was satisfied that her son got good grades and was content playing Tomb Raider and Final Fantasy VII on Sony Playstation. Girls were a thought on Justin's mind but it hadn't gotten to the point where they were calling or coming over yet. She was satisfied for now but Pat knew that any day now, she'd come home and find Justin sitting on the sofa with some girl who'd be all teeth smiling at her, trying to be her best friend just to get closer to her son.

On my way out of the office I piled the disarray of papers into one neat stack and said a little prayer that tonight would go off without a hitch.

"The Moore account, Terry." I smile as I hand the designs with a little post-it note to fax to the San Fernando office.

"What are you so happy about, Lea?" she asks with a puzzled-suspicious look on her face.

"It's Friday," I mouthed.

"Have a nice weekend, Terry."

"You too, Lea," she said shaking her head and smiling.

Terry is our friendly secretary. She's soft- spoken, dedicated and she runs my errands without complaining. I delivered my goodnights on the way out as I debated whether or not to go to the dental office.

"Goodnight, Lea," the guys at the water cooler say in harmony. Jack, Will and Darren, fine specimens. Jack and Will were brothers, tall and handsome. Darren had relocated from the California office. They were the objects of affection for at least a dozen women who worked in the office building. I smiled and waved goodnight. I was content, I belonged to Mark, heart, mind and soul. No one else could compare. I'm in love.

I wasn't in the mood for the dentist tonight; it would only sidetrack me from my plans. I had to conjure every sensual thought that I could. I needed to create an atmosphere. I smoothed out my skirt that held wrinkles now because I had been sitting all day. I walked out of the building thinking that this was the only thing I disliked about linen, it wrinkled too easily. I had chosen this navy linen skirt suit because it was comfortable, not just because Mark liked it. I tried to remember off of the top of my head how many candles I had left in my stash back at the apartment. I think I still had three from the Candle Barn, they were vanilla scented, but I needed more than three to create the mood I was after tonight.

Sometimes I felt so awkward to be wearing braces at twenty-eight. Braces are a teenage thing I used to think, but now I understand that nowadays it's more about perfecting what you have. I tried to distract myself from tonight and what I anticipated happening between us. I couldn't wait to kiss him, to caress him and to make him feel as special as I feel right now thinking about him. Tonight, I couldn't wait. Ecstasy had a name, Mark.

I would definitely reschedule my dental appointment. What I have to say to Mark, or ask him rather, was hard enough without having my teeth shifting in my mouth when I'm trying to say it. The girl at the dental office was pleasant. Her name was Michelle. Cell phones do come in handy; they aren't always for show. Well, at least mine wasn't, I thought as I jotted the date my appointment was rescheduled for on a scrap piece of paper and stuffed it down into my bag.

"Please be open, please be open," I say to the bank as I weave in and out of the people who seem to be walking like they are sightseeing. They should make all tourists wear tee shirts that say "Hey, look at me; this is my first time in New York," I think as I slide right past the security guard at the bank just as he's about to pull the door and lock up.

"There is a God," I say as I think to myself. "What are security guards for anyway?" I mean, when someone robs a bank they have to get on the floor like the rest of us. It's not like they have some formal training that teaches them how to cope in a bank heist. I guess having guards just makes the bank look like it's protected, under surveillance or impenetrable or something.

I wonder if I'm the only one who wonders about the silly things in life like who made up the idea of lines? Was there just one person standing somewhere and then someone else came up behind them and said, "Do you mind if I stand here too?" You stand on a line to cash a check, to ask a question, to board a bus, to get your own money out of the bank and to buy a loaf of bread. I think that there are too many lines and too many rules and regulations, and I also think that I think too much. I only get obsessive with my thinking when I'm nervous.

"Okay, I'm nervous. Calm down, Lea," I tell myself.

I stand waiting for an available room to view the contents of my safety deposit box, and my mind wanders some more. "How safe are my valuables in here anyway?" Once I'm inside I always panic thinking that when I open my box it will be empty, or that people are secretly trying to find out what I have in here. Evidence that I watch too much TV. But as the woman that was ahead of me comes out of the viewing room, I go in and have a seat at the table, the bank secretary bring my box, and as usual inside, safe and sound, are my only treasures that I have managed to store up on earth. A few savings bonds, my passport, my birth certificate, *"our"* engagement rings and my diamond earrings.

I take the earrings out of their case and they sparkle, the way that good quality diamonds are supposed to. They're sensational, .75 carats each. I'm nervous and I have butterflies in my stomach, thinking to myself that this is really going to happen. He'll say yes. I know he will. When I put him on the spot or catch him off guard, a lot of champagne, I know the drill. He'll know I'm serious and he'll give up without a fight, or maybe he'll just say yes because deep down he loves me too. He always wants to talk. Talk, talk, talk. Enough talking, time for some action.

Once I get home, and run a mile or two on the treadmill to work up a sweat and work off what I didn't eat today, I'll sink into a luxurious bath and have a mimosa to calm me down a bit. I picked up my dry cleaning, playing over and over again in my mind what tonight would be like.

I stop and get a bunch of fresh yellow roses from the fruit stand at the corner and a half-gallon of orange juice. I make mental notes all the way home. Everything had to be perfect.

Enjoying the warm air and the aroma of cultural dishes mingling together, my hurry turns into a stroll and I relax a little as the sun goes down. I pick up a few fragrant candles at the Wax Motif and I'm home, finally. With no time to sort through the mail, I find there's really no need because I can already guess what the postman brought me today. A mailbox full of catalogs. Neiman Marcus, J. Crew, Tweeds, Pastille, One 212, Essence and Bloomingdale's by Mail.

I liked J.Crew the best, not because their clothes were the most expensive but because they were quality. I'm a quality girl, I tried convincing myself. I don't fall in love with a label. So I skim through loads of catalogs that I've probably ordered out of maybe once and now they keep sending them, along with magazines that I didn't even want to subscribe to, to kill some time, but mostly to cover up my nervousness. The trick with these magazine publishers is to tell you that the first issue is free. But when you forget to write cancel on the bill and send it back, they rush and send you another issue so that you're obligated to pay for the entire subscription.

Then they send you a second notice statement asking, "Is there a problem?" I always say that one day I'll write back and say, "Yes, the problem is that I never wanted to subscribe to your magazine, I just wanted to get the one free issue and the free CD or video, so now stop writing me!" I wonder if they actually get letters like that. I can't imagine that someone would have the nerve.

I check my machine, "Number of messages: zero" and I can't believe that I don't even get a pep talk from Sasha or Josai about tonight. You would think that they would call to see if I was fine, nervous or excited since they are the only ones I've told about the master plan and have sworn to secrecy. Nia was too wrapped up in Freddie to hear about my love life, and Patricia seems to be on a second honeymoon of sorts with Sean. So I had confided in my two oldest friends. Thinking about how I'm feeling about tonight, I realize that I'm all of the above. I'm fine, nervous and excited as I slip into something a little more comfortable, a pair of sweats and my March of Dimes tee shirt that I was awarded when I proudly went the distance in the walk-a-thon and took in over $100 in pledges.

I'm fine I convince myself because I can handle it. I'm nervous because this is a 'til death do you part thing. And I'm excited because for once I'm standing up and doing something that I want to do and not just waiting for someone to give me his green light of approval. Anticipating tonight, I realize I really don't feel like sweating and I don't feel like exerting much energy now, so I climb down off of the treadmill breathing a sigh of relief. Though I didn't exert an ounce of energy. I need to save that for later on tonight, I justified.

I walked over to the mirror examining my face and skin. I brushed, wrapped, pinned and sprayed my hair so it would hold, spritzed on a little shine and headed for the bathroom. I began to fill the bathtub with water as warm as my body can take, as warm as Mark's arms around me and his flesh against my flesh, as warm as his breath breathing on my neck and his warm-blooded hands roaming wherever they please. As warm as waking up in the sun together on the beach, as warm as a hot water bottle in just the right spot. I pour a little *Calyx* bath gel in the bath hoping that it will fill the house with a sweet fragrance that will linger until we return tonight.

I'm on plural mode, I think, as I arrange the tiny yellow rosebuds, that are about a day from blooming, in an

19

exquisite **Mikasa** crystal vase that was a birthday present from Mark the year before last. I placed them on the diningroom table. Flowers do something to a room. They breathe life and happiness. They evoke change. I pinned back the lace curtains so that the slight breeze could blow through the house.

I laid out my dress, my lingerie and the earrings on my bed. What possessed me to buy a leopard print comforter with matching sheets is beyond me. I guess the purpose was to match the leopard skin covered chair by the window that I never sit in. I think Nia talked me into getting that chair. "The girl was wild," I laughed to myself, and I was a loyal fan. Digging around in the closet for my favorite strappy sandals, I only find one, which means that when I was away on business my sister Nicky was over here in my stuff.

I think I'm borderline compulsive. My closet is semi-organized but I still know where everything is. I rummage under a few shopping bags and boxes in the back of the closet and find the other sandal under a lace teddy. My favorite black lace teddy. That means she was having sex in my apartment too. I could imagine her dancing around for whoever he was in my lace teddy and sandals. You'd think she'd at least wash it. I'll call her tomorrow and let her have it, because this isn't a motel. Tomorrow, because today is too precious to ruin.

I pulled out two of my seldom-used pieces of stemware and mixed a quick mimosa. I sip on it as I head for the bathroom. Maybe Mark would like a little taste when he got here. It was sweet with a hint of tartness. Just how I liked it. Slowly I reach a state of total euphoria as I settle down into my warm bath. The scent of flowers and pink grapefruit fill the air. I turn on the water, making it almost hotter than I can stand. If he only knew how much trouble went into making this day perfect he would understand just how much he means to me. For six years I've held back, and I'm all tuckered out from restraining my feelings and myself.

I'm up to my neck in a soothing bath, when the phone rings. It never fails that as soon as I get settled into my bath the telephone rings. It's just like whenever I blow-dry my hair, I imagine I hear the telephone too. Well, whoever it is will have to wait until I'm done and that won't be any time soon, I think, as I play with little bubbles and splash the water with my toes. It's only six-thirty. Mark and I hadn't even talked and I was already making mental wedding plans. Lavender and salmon rosebuds. Lots of them. Bunches. The most fabulous Vera Wang wedding gown and a custom made headpiece. Something long and flowing. But what would our children look like? Would they have curly hair like Mark or fairer hair, like me? I wonder if the little girl or boy would be beautiful enough to be a model, I think as I begin to drift off. Will they be on television, acting? Or commercials? By the time they're all grown up, underwear ads will be passe.

"Mommee can I have a cookie?"

"You just ate breakfast, Zoe."

"So, why can't I have a cookie then?"

"Because you'll burst, that's why."

"Don't look at me with that sad face, girl."

"Mommeee?"

"Okay, have some grapes."

"I don't like seeds," she'll pout."

"They make me choke."

"Grapes are good for you, besides these don't have seeds."

"What do they have mommee?"

"What does what have?"

"The grapes, you said they're good for you, what do they have?"

"Iodine."

"Iodine?"

"Yes, here."

"Mommee, what time is the party?"

"Three o'clock, Zoe."

"Do you think everyone will come, Mommee?"

"Yes girl, now go upstairs and wake your father."

"Mommee he's already woke," she said. "He's on the computer with Jada."

"Tell your father that he has to pick up the cake before twelve and get the hot dogs too."

"Burgers too, right mommee?"

"Yes burgers too, but we already have burgers in the freezer."

"Good, because I like burgers, mommee."

"Do mommy a favor and bring your sister downstairs when you go up, Zoe."

A life with children, Mark's children, is something that I've envisioned over and over again in my mind. After feeling myself dozing off for about the second or third time, I let the water out of the bathtub before I drowned. Tomorrow's headlines would read, "Drunk woman found dead in bathtub, details at eleven." Moma would have a fit. Standing up to reach for the towel, I can feel the effects of the champagne. Carefully, I step out of the tub onto my pile of clothes and dry myself off. I slather on moisturizer, thinking that tonight will be perfect. Perfect.

I always walk around my house naked. I've never really thought much of it, until now. I like being naked, not because I'm an exhibitionist, but, because I have five robes in fabrics from satin to denim, and when I take a bath I always forget to bring one in with me. Anyway it's liberating. After living with three sisters and a brother for so many years, it's nice to know that this is my place and I can do whatever whenever I want.

The number one was flashing on my machine. Probably Josai or Sasha calling to check on me after all. I'm not in the mood for "Are you sure you want to do this?" I'm a grown woman, I know what I want to do. You'd think I was doing something drastic, detrimental to my health or illegal. If they want to pep talk me, it's fine, but otherwise I'm not calling them back. Not tonight anyway.

I was dying to see how the whole outfit would pull together when the doorbell rang. "Hey, Nia."

"What's going on, Lea?" she asks, wearing her famous black leggings and an animal print top tied into a knot right above her belly.

"I've got a date."

"Oh really?"

"Yes."

"Why, what's wrong, Nia?"

"Nothing, I just thought we could sit around and talk. Freddie wants to come by, but I don't know. I'm not in the mood for his stuff. He's been in a bad mood all week."

"Girl you know you love that man."

"Yes, I do love him, but sometimes I need a break! I don't want attitude tonight. Do you know what I mean?"

"I sure do."

"We need a girl's night out. No men, and good food."

"Yeah, that's right Lee, lots of good food!"

"That's what I'm talking about."

"We need to get together. You, me, Pat and the rest of the girls."

"Okay, it's a plan."

"Great."

"But I've got to get ready girl. I don't want to be late."

"Okay, okay. You go on, Lea. Enjoy yourself."

"Thanks for stopping by, I'll let you know how it goes tonight, girl."

"Who are you going out with anyway?"

"Mark."

"Oh, I see..."

"What's wrong with that?"

"Nothing, I just thought that you said that he was preoccupied or something."

"He is. With me," I smile.

"Oh, okay," she nods.

"See you later, Lee."

"I'll call you, Nia."

"Sure you will."

"I promise!"

"Okay, okay, have fun."

"I will," I giggle to myself.

I put on my pewter unmentionables and slip on the dress. Crepe wears well. I smooth out every crease and wrinkle, though there aren't many because I fill the dress, and it fits like a glove. I take the pins out of my hair and it sort of falls neatly around my face, I want to look a little uninhibited and inviting tonight so I bend over, shake my hair, like the white girls do. It looks good; I'll leave it like that.

It's seven-thirty; Mark will be here soon. He is my soul mate, if there is such a thing. When I envision our life together I see dinner parties, skiing in Aspen and spoiled rotten children who get Porsches on their sixteenth birthday. It's nice to have a career and be able to contemplate having things in life. I mean I have friends who work at jobs that pay them a little over minimum wage and I try to convince them, or her rather, to go back to school. I don't like to name names; I just want to see women, Sasha in particular, do more for herself.

Sometimes I think that she is just a little jealous of me. I mean, we are friends and all, but I go out and buy whatever my heart desires and she still has to rely on lay-away plans and this man giving her twenty dollars and the other man giving her forty. So, what does that say about her? Lord knows that I have no problem when it comes to lending to someone in need, and she is my girlfriend, but we need goals, not handouts.

We need to choose our men carefully. Fine is good, but fine can't pay the bills. You can't live in light green eyes and you can't drive a pair of Tommy Hilfiger boxers. "But, I've been to college," she says.

"Where's the proof? Where's the degree?" I ask her. Sure it's only a piece of paper but without it you don't have a leg to stand on. It's been an ongoing debate. But I won't let that worry me tonight because I'm in the mood for love.

I'm craving a little Maxwell. He's bad and he's blowing up the airwaves. I put on "Don't Ever Wonder." That's my groove. I press repeat. I slip on the watch and the earrings and check the phone to see who had the audacity to call and interrupt my destiny in the making. I called Mark first to see if he'd left to come over yet, his machine picks up. In a deep baritone "Barry White-ish" voice he croons, "Hey, I'm sorry I missed you, leave me a message after the beep, peace." I hang up.

Sometimes I call when I know he's not there just to listen to his voice on the machine. Crazy? I guess, but I can bet that I'm not the only one. Sometimes when I come in, my machine says zero messages and then even though the last person I talked to the night before wasn't him, his number comes up on my caller ID. Modern technology, what would we do without it?

I press the playback button. "Number of messages: one."

"Lea, this is Mark, don't be mad but I have to cancel tonight. I have an emergency and I can't get into it right now. Don't be upset, there will be other times, okay? I'll call you tomorrow."

Chapter Three

It had to be about 11:00 P.M. and I sloshed around the apartment with a bottle in one hand and bitter regret in the pit of my stomach. I got angry, furious, pissed off, felt violated and betrayed. We've been playing this game too long and I was sick of it! Maybe he was gay like my friends said. Since when does a woman have to go out and buy a ring for a man anyway?

I was on my second bottle of champagne and I was rummaging around in the junk closet. I pulled out a few old canvases from my post-pottery but "I'm-still-creative" days, and I pried the lids off of a few cans of acrylic paints. I took off my watch and earrings, slipped off my sandals and got "buck wild." I started slinging paint across the old dusty canvas. Royal blue, green and black, I scratched at it and punched it, taking out all of my anger, frustration, passion, revenge, lust and hate on it.

"Who does he think he is?" Paint flying, blue and green but mostly red in my hair and on my face.

"Standing me up?" I was slipping and sliding on paint, barely able to catch my balance. The colors were everywhere, and there I was standing in the middle of my dining room looking at what he created. So, I dubbed it

26

"Mark's Mess." I was gonna send it to him when I was done. This painting was my interpretation of what he had done to me. He foiled my plan and he destroyed my life. It wasn't the first time either. Tears began streaming down my face and I had no one to comfort me. No one.

I took a much-needed break. I was exhausted. It was midnight now. The moon was full and the stars were dancing in the sky, but it was humid and I was sticky and dizzy. I didn't need any more alcohol but since I wasn't in the mood or in my right mind to determine what was good for me, I popped the cork on another bottle. More paint and another canvas later there was "Hurricane Mark" that was created between one and two in the morning. Red madness on canvas with two eyes looking helplessly from within scratch lines and mayhem.

I'm going to call my sister, Nicky, first thing in the morning, right after I change my phone number. Yes, he had pushed me that far. First thing in the morning I'm going to call the phone company and have my phone number changed. A non-published number. Mumms. The most important date of my life and he cancels, so, here I am drowning my sorrows in a bottle of Mumms. Three bottles to be exact. I was on the second bottle and rapidly working my way to the third. I didn't know I could drink so much. The champagne was to be celebratory. What was I celebrating? Being alone? Forever?

I stumbled over to the mirror to admire what was left of me. What I had become, what I had let him make me into. One false move and he had destroyed my whole life. How weak was I anyway? I kept mumbling oddities. I know I'm just drunk because I don't even like cheese and here I was searching the refrigerator for some. I only buy cheese for company. I looked in the mirror and I smiled. I'm not drunk I said, trying to keep my head up straight and my eyes wide open. My black crepe dress from **Byblos** looked like a Halloween costume now. My hair and my apartment were a wreck, and yep, I'm drunk.

"Rhonda, wuzzup?"

"Lea?"

"Yeah, it's Lea!"

"What's wrong with you, girl?"

"Not a thing, sis, not a thing."

"So why do you sound like you've been drinking?"

"Because I had a glass of wine a minute ago."

"A glass of wine? You sound like you've had a gallon."

"Hee-hee, you're so funny Rhonda. So...whatcha doin'?"

"Waiting for this no good husband of mine to come home."

"Well, where did he go?"

"He said he was working late, but I called the office and as usual there's no answer."

"Child, leave him! You don't need that, a man running around on you and making you look like a fool."

"Yeah, Lea, that's a wonderful idea but where am I going to live? In the streets?"

"Girl you need a life and a man that will treat you right."

"Moma said to give him a chance, Lea."

"Give him a chance to what? Do it again?"

"No, to change, Aaliyah. That's something you wouldn't understand. When you make a commitment to someone you don't just throw in the towel that easily."

"Well, girl, it sounds like you made a commitment to him and he made a commitment to the whole female population. Hee-hee."

"Thanks a lot, Lea."

"Nah, sis, I didn't mean that how it sounded."

28

"Sure you didn't." I'm sorry, Rhonda, but you know that you can come and stay with me girl.

"I'll think about it Lea."

"Okay girl. Look I've gotta run...sis."

"What's the hurry, Lea? You're always running someplace."

"I've got a date."

"A date?"

"Yeah, a date!"

"At 2:00 A.M.?" I was silent.

"Okay, Lea, but lay off the wine."

"Hee-hee, okay Ra-Ra, byeeee."

I'm usually a light sleeper. I used to hear my brother trying to sneak in my room when I was little, trying to stick something in my ear or tickle my feet so I'd wake up. That's probably why I still sleep with the covers over my head and tucked under my feet, except for last night. I hung up from Rhonda, fell face down on the bed and got the paint that was all over my dress and hair on my comforter and my pillowcases. I tried to focus on the clock on the dresser that looked like it was saying 2:57 p.m.

I practically slept through the whole day. I wish I could sleep through my whole life and just wake up when it's time for the rapture or something. And as if what I remembered from last night wasn't enough, I dreamt I was in jail with a fat lady and she wasn't singing, she wouldn't stop crying so I gave her a turkey sandwich and then she started screaming. That had to be symbolic of something. Maybe I'm always giving somebody something and they don't appreciate it. Maybe it was a reference to Mark. The number five was flashing on my answering machine now and I didn't care. I stumbled to the bathroom and washed my face and brushed my teeth. I didn't feel like flossing this morning, so I didn't. I called the phone company. I lied. I told that annoying little robotic sounding woman I had been getting prank calls for the past three months at two in the morning.

She wanted to know why I hadn't reported it sooner. "I thought it would eventually stop," I said. I guess I sounded pretty convincing but the order department still had me on hold for about forty-five minutes. They wanted to verify my address and social security number and they wanted to know where I worked.

"I don't remember going through all of this before," I told her.

"We have a lot of new procedures in place," she said, trying to sell me repair insurance and caller ID.

"I already have caller ID," I told her.

"All I want is what I had before," I said. I wait some more, this was time consuming, and I had things to do. I finally wrote down my new number. I dialed Nicky's number.

"Hello, Nicky?"

"Hey, Lee, what's up?"

"My patent leather sandals, girl."

"Lee, I only borrowed them for one date."

"My lace teddy?"

"Lee, give me a break. I house-sat for you, the least you could do is let me borrow your stuff!"

She couldn't be serious. I calmed myself down.

"All I ever want you to do is ask first, Nicole!"

"You weren't there, Aaliyah!"

We always called each other by our full first names when we were upset with each other.

"Anyway I didn't call for that."

"So why did you call?"

"I want you to come and get some things that I want to get rid of."

"Like what?"

"Like my diamond studs and some outfits."

"Why, Lee?"

"Why what?"

"Why are you giving them away?"

"Do you want them or not, Nick?"

"Yes!" She always says that coming over to my place was like going shopping, she always went home with something, and I don't mind giving her things because I know that she will wear and appreciate them.

"Take down my new number, too."

"Okay, Lee, but, tell me what's wrong? Why did you change your number?"

"Nick, I'm going out tonight and you have the keys so just let yourself in. The earrings are on the dresser. I'll leave the clothes out for you and I'll talk to you later."

"Lee?"

"Bye, Nicky."

Even though she's my sister and I'm not that much older than she is, I still don't like to dump on her. I don't like to dump on anyone for that matter. I just try and cope. Some people don't care, they just dump and dump on you until they feel better and you're miserable. I wasn't like that.

I called Joe. She wasn't home, I left my new number on her machine and I called my Moma and gave her the new number and chatted with her for a few. She had started taking leisurely walks through the neighborhood.

"Be careful in the sun Moma. It's no good to get too much sun."

"I'll be fine. I go out early in the morning before it gets too hot." I always send Moma money when I can, even though I know that when I do she wires some of it to that no-good, baby-making Todd, which angers me very much. But, I have to do for my Moma. She loved her son, and I loved him, too. I just wish he'd get a job.

James is an artist. He said if I ever decided to take painting seriously to let him know. I wouldn't call what I had done Van Gogh or Degas, but I've seen crap that looked worse than this on exhibit in the Metropolitan Museum of Art and the Guggenheim.

"James? It's Lea."

"Hey lady, what's happening?"

"Nothing much. I have some things that I would like you to come and take a look at whenever you have the time."

"Like what things?"

"Art."

"Art?"

"Yes, art."

"Well, when can I come by?"

"Whenever you get a chance, there's no rush."

"Can I come by now? I'm not busy."

"Umm, well, give me about an hour or two, I have to run a few errands. I'll be back soon."

"Okay, Lea. Oh, Lea, I have a friend here with me, is it okay if I bring him?"

"The more the merrier," I said.

It had to be about eighty-five degrees outside. I had a slight hangover. It felt like a tiny man was in my head playing the drums. I opened every window in the house, put a little cinnamon in a pot of boiling water to freshen up the place, and then gathered the paint cans together to throw into the incinerator, even though you're not really supposed to. But there was no way I was walking down from the eleventh floor to put them in the recyclable bin out back, or getting on the elevator with these dripping paint cans either. If they want to give me a ticket they'll have to prove it was me first.

I had gotten paint on the walls, the windows, the ceiling and all over the rug. Thank God it was an area rug; I can roll it up and take it to the dry cleaners early Monday morning. I can just imagine how much they will want to charge me to get the stains out, and all because I was too drunk and lazy to use a dropcloth or common sense. But then that's what happens when you lose control. I looked at my two masterpieces, "Mark's Mess" and "Hurricane Mark." And I guessed it was beginning to sound obsessively redundant to keep using Mark's name. I can't ever get over him if I don't allow myself to forget.

The thing is that this is not the first time that he disappointed me. You'd think that I would be used to it by now. I took a nice relaxing shower and washed the paint out of my hair. I still had a couple of red streaks when I was done, but it was going to have to stay that way until my appointment at **Black Roots** Monday evening, although I dreaded having to go way out to Brooklyn. But, Evelyn is the best and she makes my hair look fabulous even when I'm not trying.

Chapter Four

Sifting through my closet I realized that I didn't own a single pair of jeans or any casual clothing. Always trying to look pretty for Mark. Trying to be the fashion model I wasn't. I pulled out a couple of dresses that Mark had suggested would look nice on me, a red linen one, a blue wool *Calvin Klein,* and a pale yellow *Jil Sander* mini rayon sundress with a matching shirt jacket. I folded them nicely and put them on the sofa for Nicky, I put the patent sandals and the black lace teddy with them. I really have a thing about wearing clothes after someone else has had them on. It irks my nerves in a royal way. It's my pet peeve. An irreversible one.

I pulled on a pair of black leggings and found a bright lime blouse that would match and a pair of comfortable black sandals. I thought I looked more like Nia now than Nia did. I put on a pair of dark shades and collected the empty bottles from around the room. If anyone saw all these bottles lying around they would think that there was a party here last night, and there was, I was just the only guest, the other guest was a no-show. I can't get over him canceling at the last minute like that. He is so insensitive. I just want to get over it and him. I needed to associate with people who respected me.

"What could he have had to do that was more important than dinner with me?" He blew off my proposal and everything.

While I sat on the sofa and gazed across the room at "Mark's Mess" and "Hurricane Mark," I figured the paintings were kind of abstract yet alluring. The phone was still blinking five. I pressed the playback button on the answering machine. Again I hear pathetic Mark with his lame excuse, "Lea, this is Mark, don't be mad but I have to cancel tonight. I have an emergency and I can't get into it right now. Don't be upset, there'll be other times, okay? I'll call you tomorrow." Then "Good morning, Lea, it's me, Mark...are you there? Well, anyway about last night, we need to talk. Call me. It's ten-fifteen, bye."

He always says that we need to talk and then when it's down to the wire he always flakes. If he is waiting for me to call him, he can wait until hell freezes over! "Lea, it's me again, can you call me? Seriously. We need to talk. It's eleven-thirty." I guess he was getting desperate. As desperate as I was two weeks ago when I went and bought him a ring. I must have been crazy.

"Hi, Lea, it's Sasha. I was wondering what you're doing today. I wanted to come over and talk to you if it's okay. It's one, call me, bye."

"Lea, it's Mark, I know you're there, please pick up the phone. Lea? I don't believe you. We can still go out tonight if you want to. Why are you taking this so seriously? Lea?" I guess he ran out of words because he hung up.

The final message was a song playing in the background, "Love is Here" by Des'ree, it was one of my favorites. He knows I love the song and I even told him I wanted to walk down the aisle to this. I knew it was him.

35

He sure knew how to push my buttons. It won't make me call him though. In the middle of the song I pressed erase. I called Sasha, the machine picked up. I left my new number. The doorbell rang. I had no time now to be emotional. It's a done deal. Besides no one liked whiny women, least of all me.

"James, how are you?" I said, lifting my shades and resting them atop my head. James was always a good-looking man, a little too tall and lanky for me but he was still a good catch. He had a goatee and a thinly- shaped mustache. He was predictable, he always brought flowers and he always wore hushpuppies, even before they became fashionable again. We tried to do a little thing in the past and it didn't work out because he wanted to smother me. Men say that they don't know what women want, but all women want is a balance. Don't act like you could care less and don't act like fatal attraction. It's simple.

We always hugged when we saw each other; he just never wanted to let go.

"Aaliyah, this is Stephen. Stephen, this is Aaliyah," James said.

"Call me Lea." I nodded approvingly.

"Call me Steve," he grinned. I giggled, feeling flirty.

"What's wrong?" he said.

"Nothing, I'm fine." I was impressed, I hope it didn't show too much. He was kind of cute, he had on a bandanna, had a buffed body and a nice smile. I loved a man with a nice smile.

"You've got a nice place here, Lea," he said, obviously trying to flatter me. He was looking at the windowsills at my more successful pieces of pottery. I thanked him for the compliment but I know that sometimes my stuff comes out looking like it fell off the wheel and then I have to add a handle and call it an Egyptian pitcher or something exotic like that.

"So, Lea, I see you've been busy," James said, looking over my two pieces of work, staring into "Mark's Mess" like he was trying to find a hidden message or make something out of my nothing. "Your work is good, Lea. The color has depth and definition and makes a very strong statement."

"What statement was that?"

I wondered. Little did he know I didn't spend ten days trying to get the lines exactly right or the color to contrast.

"What type of brushes did you use?"

"Uh, sable," I said, too embarrassed to tell this artistically-inclined man that I used my fingers and hands to craft what he seems to think is a great masterpiece.

"It's not completely dry yet. I was working on it early this morning."

"What do you think, Steve?" James asked.

"I like it," he said, looking around. He was beginning to look like he was casing the joint. At that instant his charm wore off.

"I can come by tomorrow to pick these pieces up. I'll take them to the gallery with my other pieces. I have a show on Wednesday at the Beekman."

"Really?" I was ecstatic but I was trying not to be too hopeful.

"I can't promise you anything but it will get your work out there and show people what you can do. We need more black artists," he said, "and your work is very good Lea."

"Thanks, James." I smiled and nodded. James had write-ups in New York magazine and in the trade papers. They say that he has style.

37

I don't know the difference between impressionist, abstract and connect the dots, but I liked to paint and I especially enjoyed it last night. It was a mental release. I felt as if all the dead weight was lifted off my back.

"The showing is scheduled for Wednesday and we'll see what gives," he said.

"Fine." I mean it's not like I'm Picasso, I thought. Most artists really weren't famous until they died. If I had to die to become famous, forget it.

"I'll call you before I come, okay?"

"Sure, James," I beamed. "It was nice to meet you Lea," Steve said, eyeing me from head to toe."

"You too, Steve, you too," I said, brushing him off after realizing how hungry he looked. The last thing I needed was another starving man. He was good-looking but you have to learn early on in life which ones have self-control and which ones are all out freaks, and right now my "he's a freak radar" was at ten. I saw them both to the door.

I'd really like to take in a movie, I thought to myself. I was bored. "The Truth About Cats and Dogs" and "Up Close and Personal" were too mushy, and I'm definitely not in the mood for kissy-kissy, mushy-mushy stuff right now. I think something like "A Thin Line Between Love and Hate" is more my speed. A black fatal attraction is what I'm feeling like right now.

I went down the hall to let Nia know how my non-date went. I had to talk to somebody. I rang her bell about seven times before I heard the latches and locks clicking on the door.

"What happened to you girl! Too much to drink?" I kidded.

She let me in the apartment and the place was dark. The curtains were drawn and the blinds were down. I turned on the light and she moved right into the shadows as I noticed that her left eye was swollen and closed shut.

38

Her fancy lashes were hanging off and I had to sort of help her pull one out so it didn't get stuck in her eye.

"What happened, Nia!" I asked, feeling silly since I already knew what had happened. That sick son-of-a-so-and-so thought she was his sparring partner.

"We had a little disagreement," she said. She had a black eye and she thinks they had a disagreement? He was twisted and demented, I thought. She had to only weigh about one hundred and ten, if that, and it appears as if he had tossed her about.

"I'll be okay," she said.

"You'll be okay?"

"Yes."

"Yes, but what about him? You better put him in jail!"

Rule number two, never get involved in another person's relationship. She wanted to allow this man to beat her to a pulp and then take him back because she loved him? Okay, Ricky Lake.

I told her to lie down on the sofa and I put ice cubes in one of her fancy dishtowels and placed it on her eye. She smiled sort of, probably more like wincing out of pain though. Her lip was split right down the middle and she had blood stains on what used to be a very pretty lilac silk pajama top. She was as beautiful as a chocolate playboy bunny and could get any man she wanted. Yet the one she wanted, thought she was merchandise. His property.

"Where is he?" I demanded.

"He left this morning."

"Well...why did he?"

"He was listening to the messages on my machine and he heard a message from a friend. He was just a friend, Lea," she began to sob uncontrollably.

"It'll be okay, girl. It doesn't matter anyway, Nia. You should be able to have men call you," I consoled her.

39

"You aren't married to Freddie. Come and go with me to a movie, girl."

"No, I don't feel like a movie now, Lea."

"C'mon, it will be good for you."

"No, thanks."

"I just want to stay here. I have to call a few clients and cancel my appointments for this week and probably the next. I can't go out looking like this."

"I know, girl. Well, do you want me to stay with you?"

"No, you go to the movies. Didn't you have a date last night?"

"Yeah, but it's not important now. You get some rest and I'll check on you later."

"Okay, girl?"

"Lea?"

"Yes?"

"Please don't tell anybody."

I bit my lip, closed my eyes and nodded my head.

"Okay, I won't. Talk to you later?"

"Okay."

I put on my knapsack and headed to the West Side to see if Sasha wanted to go with me. I couldn't shake the frightened look that Nia had in her eyes and the way she broke down in hysterical tears explaining what had happened. I decided by the time I got to the lobby of my building to go alone. I mean I'm really not in the mood for a whole lot of questions, just like I was sure Nia wasn't. After all I don't want people to feel sorry for me, I can take care of myself. They say that misery loves company but not me. Just leave me alone and I'll be fine. I guess that's sort of what Nia was feeling right now. She was more like me than I'd like to admit. She was in love with a man that treated her like dirt.

Chapter Five

Sony theaters had wide unobstructed aisles and great munchies. I wasn't about to undo all the exercise I've been doing by pigging out but, popcorn with extra butter, bonbons, a cherry arctic blast and a giant hot dog with ketchup and mustard were calling my name. Right in front of me was a couple kissing and openly displaying affection, portions of which were best left for the bedroom. They couldn't even wait until it got dark. It wasn't too crowded in the theater, that's why I liked to come early in the day and leave the wild nights to the youngsters.

I liked Lynn Whitfield but I didn't care much for Martin Lawrence. She's the only reason I'm seeing this movie. I mean, he gets a chuckle out of me every now and then but for the most part he's downright corny. I hope they cancel his show because he's stupid. The funniest part of his show was Sha-Ne-Neh but he hardly ever does her anymore or the little snotty-nosed boy.

This was a what-goes-around-comes-around movie and the guy in the movie reminded me of Mark. He only wanted a woman until he knew he had her and then...see ya! Using those lame one- liners like, "Baby, are your legs

41

tired? Because you've been running through my mind all night" and "Do you have a quarter? Because my mother said to call her when I fell in love." If women fall for that, or even think that it's cute when these men say it, then they deserve every single second of heartache that they get.

You could tell that Martin produced this film, it's full of profanity. But, he was foul-mouthed on Def Comedy Jam and he pushes the limits on his show, so I guess you should expect the same thing from him in a movie. He can't even act. Bobby Brown did a better job at acting than he did. He got what he deserved though. I'm glad that as a single black woman that I don't have to resort to using little four and three letter words to get my point across. That's where articulation and education come in. There were thousands of adjectives out there; it never made sense to me that most people limited themselves to the four letter ones.

A black fatal attraction. It always amazed me that when we see white people starring in movies, that we would do things differently than they do because we are black. But the reality is that we are all the same and that some of us make the same decisions that they make and some of us don't. Lynn Whitfield looks fabulous as always. Her clothes were wearing her well. Everything was flowing like she should be wearing *Calyx* or something.

I'm on this *Calyx* kick after reading this book by an author whose books keep being turned into movies, and all she kept raving about in this last book was *Calyx, Calyx, Calyx*. She poured *Calyx* here and rubbed *Calyx* there, and her man kept saying how she smelled good throughout the whole book. I though it was just hype, or that maybe they paid her to mention it twenty times and endorse their product like they did with Elizabeth Taylor and her new fragrance on all the sitcoms that she guest starred on.

I treated myself to a sample and ended up buying the whole set. It smells fabulous, in a sensual kind of way.

The effect it had when I entered a room was existential and I liked it. People smiled as you walked by and they got a hint of it. As if to say, hey that's nice. It's nice to be appreciated though. Even if it was only for how you smelled.

I stomped out of the theater, upset because of how the movie ended. It seemed that he got off the hook scott free, and I came to the conclusion that women give men power, and the minute we exert a little authority of our own and try to receive some of the power we gave them back, we are labeled sexist and men bashers. But label me what you want, I say. But for clarity, if you're a dog then bark, and if you're a man act like one. It's not like I hate men but spare me all the details, it's just that sometimes life isn't very funny, especially not mine.

It was only ten o'clock, and even though I'm not desperate, I'd really like someone to talk to. So, I decided to head on over to Sasha's. We could talk and fix something to eat at her house since I don't feel like cooking or looking at any more painted messes. I could barely get in her building with all the kids blocking the entrance. Brothers hovering in front of the building waiting for anything with breasts and legs to walk by just so they could try and kick it to her, and if she dared not respond, then they'd hurl the 5 letter word at her. Pathetic. Go to bed I wanted to tell them, that's exactly why they're trying to implement a curfew because these kids wandered around too much and ended up getting into trouble.

Most of them had no supervision. What was a nine-year old doing hanging out in the park at ten o'clock at night? It wasn't even really a park because the swings were missing and the slide looked like someone threw up on it. I would like to know what their mothers say when they sit upstairs watching re-runs of "Roseanne," and the "It's ten o'clock. Do you know where your children are?" ad comes on. That's when they probably get up and make a sandwich or something. It seems that they could care less about their kids. Whenever I visit Sasha, I hate it! I must be more desperate than I thought. I'm always afraid that I'll get stuck in her rickety elevator. That's why I hardly visit. The buttons were burned and partially melted, I counted and pressed what I guessed was seven. I took it up to seven and I rang Sasha's doorbell.

"Sasha? You don't look too good, girl, are you okay?"

"No, I'm not feeling well," she says." Sasha was fair-skinned and had lips that were lightly darkened because she smoked. Her eyes were large enough, besides the fact that she wore contacts and had to widen her eyes to see through them.

"I got your message, Sasha," I said, as I stood in the hall getting the impression that she didn't want to let me in.

"Uh, can I come in?"

"Oh, sure, sure, come in. Um, Lea...I need to talk to you."

"Good, I need to talk to you, too. Let me tell you what that clown Mark did to me last night. And please don't tell me 'I told you so'."

"Me first, Lea. I want to tell you..."

"No, Sasha, let me finish. I planned everything down to the lingerie, girl, and he stood me up!"

I went on. "Always telling me about family problems in Phillie."

"Lea, I'm pregnant."

"Pregnant? What? You're not even seeing anyone are you?"

"Well, sort of, I mean... Trust me, I never meant for any of this to happen, Lea."

"We never do, girl" I console. "But are you going to keep it?"

"Yes, I'm keeping it. I love him and he loves me."

"You keep saying him, him who Sasha?" My voice echoed as my vision of perfection emerged from her bedroom and my heart, my soul and my life was snatched right out from under me.

"Mark?" He stood there looking like a lost sheep. Like he had strayed from the herd. Like he was finally busted. My breathing became shallow and my legs felt numb. My heart pounded like someone who was being chased. Anger invited itself and surged through me.

"I'm the family problem," Sasha said, not even wearing a look of regret. Well, she sort of looked sorry, but then again she always did. And it wasn't enough for me.

"I don't even want to know what's going on here!" I yelled. I'm in control, I tried to convince myself. I took a few deep breaths and decided that I could totally freak or handle it in private. I opted for privacy. I didn't say another word. I dared not even give him the satisfaction, or her either for that matter. I gave him a look that should have killed him dead right on the spot.

"Lea!" Mark called after me as I left. "Lea!"

Chapter Six

Family problems in Phillie. "I'm Phillie, Lea. I'm the family problem" is what Sasha had said. It was echoing in my head now. All the late nights, broken promises and interrupting calls that forced us to cancel plans, was Sasha. She was the roadblock, the detour, the stumbling stone, and the prone-to-drifting tumbleweed. And when I fabricated stories about intimacy between me and Mark, she probably laughed her funny-shaped head off because she knew, that just like the bears in Goldilocks, someone was sleeping in her bed. And that someone was Mark.

I had to occupy my mind and I knew that there was always something open in the village, a shoe store, and an eatery. I tried to take my mind off of the hell on earth that I was experiencing. I wandered up and down West 8th Street, and over to St. Mark's Place. Straight couples, gay couples and people who were pondering possibly becoming a couple, were holding hands and enjoying each other's company, I grinned. At least they had the nerve to want to take the next step, and they had a place where they fit in. Lord knows we all need a place. We need a safety zone.

My lover slash best friend betrayed me for my girlfriend. Well, I guess I should just call up Montel and see if he'd bring us on the show because when you hurt someone this deeply the whole world deserves to know about it. And to think, I wanted this man forever. I was totally considering letting this man who impregnated my best friend be my first. "Lorena Bobbett, right on girl!"

You had the right idea and the nerve to follow through. Lorena was like the Harriet Tubman of female emotion. We all talked about keeping it in a jar under the bed but I guess none of us took it as seriously as Lorena did.

On my way upstairs, the elevator stopped on ten. Justin walked on with a girl. A pretty black girl with tight jeans and a crop top. He was hugging her around her low waist until he saw me.

"Hi, Ms. Lea," he said as they lowered their heads and walked onto the elevator.

"This is going up, Justin," I said, making a mental note to have a talk with his mother as soon as possible.

"I know, it's okay," he said. Then again, let him have his fun, I thought. But what if this girl ended up pregnant like Sasha? I would have been the one who could have stopped it. I'd call Pat tomorrow.

I was depressed and upset. It was a weird feeling and I really didn't know how to handle it. I also honestly didn't know that Nicky would be here when I got back either. And I especially hoped that she wouldn't be. But, then again that's Nicky. I told her that I would leave the things for her. If I say, you have the key, then that means help yourself, not wait for me. Besides I wasn't in the mood to talk to anyone. I didn't want to see anyone's face. She was sitting on the couch next to the pile of things I had left for her, smiling, "Thanks, sis."

I don't know why she calls me that because we've never really been close. She calls me that when she wants something. We just tolerate each other. I mean, she is my sister but we're not tight. She's nineteen, and she's a selfish spoiled brat. Moma had her that way. She was never as strict on her as she was on Rhonda, Cheyenne, and me. She was the baby.

The paintings were propped up by the dining room table, and Nicky with her nosy self had already looked at them I'm sure. She tried to play it off by asking me, "What's that?"

"Art," I said.

"Well, I know that, but I wanted to know what it was supposed to be or who did it or something." "Look, Nicky, I'm not in the mood, I'm tired."

"It's only eleven-thirty, girl. Let's watch *Red Shoe Diaries*.'" She flips the channel, and I hear the tune in my head and the red shoes slide across the floor, but I'm not in the mood to re-live anyone's fantasies, especially since mine have all died.

Exotic-looking women with lipo-sucked bodies having sex in the rain with the pool man and the maid. No, I'm definitely not in the mood. But I microwave some Pop Secret and watch it with her anyway. She sat there the whole time, making lustful sounds with her mouth and kept elbowing me every other minute.

"Watching other people having sex does not turn me on," I told her.

"So why do you watch the show then, Aaliyah?"

I didn't dare tell her that I only watch it and fantasize that the people in the scene are me and Mark, and as we rub each other's bodies down with scented oils and make love by the fireplace, people are actually watching us and we are tender, we are beautiful, it's real and it lasts forever. Or at least for the half-hour.

She seemed satisfied that the show had ended as it did, but I was just glad it ended. She gathered up her things and thanked me again for her mini-shopping spree.

"Where are you coming from at this time of night anyway?" she questioned.

"I'm the oldest. Don't question me."

"Jesus, I was just asking."

"Bye, Nicky, I have a headache."

"Okay, okay, I'm going. I'll call you tomorrow, okay, Lee?"

"Okay."

As soon as Nicky left, I noticed the machine blinking two and I felt kind of sorry for brushing her off the way I did. I pressed the machine.

"Lea," Sasha says, sounding tearful and dramatic, "I just wanted to say I'm sorry and that this wasn't planned and...and." Spare me, I say. I tuned it out. "Blah, blah, blah," is all I heard.

"You can both drop dead," I say out loud as she's rambling on about friendship and forever. Mark probably made her call. The second message was Josai.

"It's ten forty-five, Lee, when you get in call me no matter what time it is, okay?" It was only 12:30 A.M. so I called her.

"Hey, Joe."

"Lea, are you okay?" There was genuine concern in her voice.

"Yes," I say, feeling the tears beginning to well up in my eyes again. I was fighting back tears, real tears, tears of pain, heartache and circumstance, I thought.

"Sasha called me and told me what happened, Lea, but I had no idea."

"Yeah, it must have been the world's best-kept secret," I said.

"How many months is she, Joe, did she say?"

"Four or five, I don't know for sure."

"She knows I bought this man a ring, Joe, why would she do this to me? Why didn't she say anything? I mean I thought that we were all supposed to be friends and the whole nine."

"You can only trust most people as far as you can throw them, Lee, you know that."

"I know," I said, sounding vulnerable. Not at all like my normal strictly-business self, but Josai listened. She was a good friend, always. She only wanted me to be happy, and up until today I was. I had found contentment in trying to make a man love me. Spending weekends being readily available, just in case he decided to call. I even considered taking him back after his no show on Friday.

"When did she develop a thing for him anyway, Joe? Huh?"

"I don't know, but, I'm coming over," she said. I didn't even try to convince her that it was too late and that it's dangerous traveling this late at night alone. I'm being selfish I know, but I'm allowed. Besides I don't want, I need, the company.

Chapter Seven

The intercom startles me. It must've been Joe. I
buzz her in. I've been on edge all week. Nervous about the
proposal and the preparation. Now I was a basket case. I'm
usually the one on the therapy and consoling side of it all,
never the victim. Joe comes bearing gifts, Hagen Daz, Lays
potato chips and People magazine. She bought flowers to
cheer me up too. I arranged the lilies in with the roses that
I bought yesterday. As we sat on the sofa, fixing our eyes on
anything in the room except each other, a deafening silence
hung there. I cleared my throat and looked down feeling
embarrassed even though the situation wasn't my fault at
all. I don't know what to say. I can't say anything. It's too
painful. It felt like open-heart surgery, where they left the
knife in by mistake. Or in this case, on purpose.

"Joe, I want to tell you something," I say, breaking
the silence, trying to muster up a little courage, and
changing the subject from the incident that had occurred
less than four hours ago. "It has absolutely nothing to do
with Mark."

"Okay, so what is it?" I get up to find a spoon to
violate my diet regimen again with a pint of pralines and

cream that has been secretly tempting me since she walked in the door.

"What is it? You know you can tell me anything," Josai says. I smile nervously.

"Remember all that stuff I said about me and Mark and rainbows and stuff?"

"Rainbows?"

"Yes, you know...umm...sex."

"Oh, yeah, what about it?"

"Well...I'm a virgin," I blurt out.

"You're a what?"

"A virgin, Joe. I've never done it before. I'm a virgin, and Mark was going to be my first, last night. I had it all planned. Champagne, Victoria's Secrets and me."

She sat there looking at me like someone had slapped her.

"Relax, Joe, it's no big deal."

"I don't believe you, girl."

"What?" I asked innocently, laughing a little but still hurting on the inside.

"You talked about seeing Stars and Stripes and hearing the Star Spangled Banner and you've never been...?"

"No, I said I saw rainbows. But I mean its not like I didn't want to or that there weren't opportunities. It's just that I was kind of saving myself, you know. I was waiting for the right time, which now it seems will never come."

"I mean if you love someone and someone loves you then you should wait, right?"

"I guess," she says. Josai was a fair-complexioned woman who had thick wavy hair that she usually kept braided in two plaits, with a part down the middle or back in a bun. She wasn't petite, but she wasn't chunky or what one would consider thick either. She looked like she had oriental mixed somewhere in her bloodline. A great catch.

She sat listening, wearing a black satin blouse and a simple silver chain with a heart charm. She had a French manicure on her neat business-length nails, and was lying back and seemed comfortable but I sensed there was something she needed to say. I couldn't take another revelation.

"I wonder if all the good-looking women will always be alone," I joked, trying to ease the tension.

"I don't know," Josai said seriously. "Maybe I'll never find anyone, maybe I'll be alone forever now," I said, beginning to feel sorry for myself all over again.

Joe hugs me and says, "It's okay, Lee."

"Here I go again," I say. My tears are evident now and she consoles me.

She looks at me and says, "You'll find someone, I really believe you will. You're cute and you can cook, girl. Men love to eat."

We grin. A seriousness comes over her again; she looks at me and smiles. She looks into my eyes with genuine concern, brushes my hair out of my face and places the strand that hangs out of place behind my ear. Then leaning forward slightly, she kisses me gently on my lips.

"Uhh, I can't do this, Joe," I say, hardly trying to resist at all, wondering if it would have been like this with Mark. She is caring, genuine and her voice whispers to me.

"I won't let anyone hurt you," she says. Her delicate touch is deliberate. There are no words exchanged between us. Yet we shared what I had never shared with anyone else in my life. Not even Mark.

Josai was sleeping now. As I look at her, I see her beautiful porcelain-like skin and wonder how I never knew that she was gay. She was plain but still feminine, she didn't wear men's shirts and boxers and she didn't chop off her hair. She was kind, generous and gentle. She worked hard, she was intelligent and she was also my friend.

Chapter Eight

I left Joe and the melted ice cream that sat in a puddle under the container on the counter. I really wasn't ready to face her this morning. Questioning me and what I did or didn't feel. I just needed someone last night. One incident didn't change who I was. I am still a man-loving woman. Last night wasn't who I was; it was just an escape. A momentary delusion of bliss, or something. A temptation of sorts. So, I browsed the bookstore like I do every Sunday, trying to make things seem normal. I was looking for nothing in particular. I just knew that I wasn't going to begin a lesbian relationship on the rebound after being hurt by a man.

I loved Mark, but sometimes everything you love is not good for you. I needed to be in the self-help section, really. Self-help was a matter of self-improvement, but I found myself in the poetry section instead. I've always had a wild fascination for poetry. Words have such meaning. I've written a few lines of verse that have been exchanged with friends who never had a negative thing to say about them. Words were powerful and I loved words, I thought as I plucked a few books from the shelf and relaxed in the reading area.

There was an old book with a burgundy cover that was tattered and somewhat torn sitting in the chair next to me. I picked up the book and put it with mine. I put my bag in the chair and noticed that the book was a very old King James Bible. It had been printed in 1898 and the pages were yellowing and fragile. Other than the worn cover and binding coming apart a little, it was in almost perfect condition. I flipped through it and although I didn't expect to see a price on it. I wondered if it belonged to someone.

I found it unusual for the bookstore to be this crowded on a Sunday. No authors were scheduled to appear, and the next book signing wasn't until the first Monday of next month. So, when people milled around and a striking thirty-something gentleman asked if he could sit next to me, I was surprised, a little reluctant, but courteous nevertheless. I glanced around the room, surveying for another empty seat he could have taken, as I moved my backpack off of the chair and held it between my legs. He quickly took a seat and leaned over towards me.

"What are you reading?" he asked, looking at my pile of books.

"Hmmm, Nikki Giovanni. Do you find her work difficult to comprehend?"

"I find her quite angry," he said.

Doesn't he have anything else to do? I look at him, and he's smiling.

"Well," I say, "poetry can be best interpreted by the author, but the reader can also interpret what a poem means to satisfy herself."

He smiled at me. He had a shy smile and beautiful teeth. I loved a man with pretty teeth.

"Well, what does that poem mean to you?" he says, as I noticed that he had no books and was focusing all of his attention directly on me. I was sure that my run on jargon would dissuade him from continuing the conversation, but it didn't. I was reading Nikki's poem, "I Wrote a Good Omelet."

"I guess you can say that this poem is liberating," I say. I had his undivided attention. "The poem is saying that when you feel love from your heart, you're not responsible for your actions. It shows that we can find meaning and love wherever we have to. We create fascination instinctively and as humans we survive by loving. We were created to find pleasure even in little things, and though we are surrounded by everyday things, love still effects our daily lives."

He listened intently, nodding his head seemingly in total agreement.

"Inside we still loved, needed and cared. Although that probably wasn't nearly what the poet intended to convey, but I guess I'll stop now." I smiled.

"That's deep," he said. "I've never heard it quite put like that before. My name is Benjamin," he offered. He was obviously trying to flatter.

"I'm Aaliyah, but some of my friends call me Lea," I said, extending my hand to his.

"Okay, Lea, you can call me Benji. Do you come here every Sunday?" he asked.

"Yes, it's a method of escape for me."

"Escape? From what?"

"Life, love, four walls," I laughed. "Do you come here often, Benji?"

"No, I was just in the neighborhood and I had some time to kiss...I mean kill...so I um." His lips curled up in the corners into a crooked smile.

"Was that a Freudian slip, Benji" I teased.

"No, no, it's just that I'm hardly ever this straightforward. I mean asking for your seat, and intruding and all." He was blushing, but rambled on anyhow. "And the fact is that I hardly ever see anyone as beautiful as you hanging out in a bookstore on a Sunday morning," he said.

"Well, it's eleven-thirty, Benji."

"Well, you know what I mean," he grinned.

I was wearing a pair of black nylon lycra pants, funky Steve Madden sandals and a lilac silk tank top with a matching lilac sweater tied around my waist. He sat with a red short-sleeved velour polo shirt and khakis. I couldn't help but smile.

"Am I making you nervous, Benji?"

"Yes...no...well...sort of."

"I'm sorry," I apologized.

"No, Lea, don't be sorry...have lunch with me."

"Lunch?"

"Yes."

"I don't know, I mean you are a stranger and you could be a maniac or something."

"Trust me, I'm no maniac," he laughed.

"Would you tell me that you were a maniac if you really were one?" I asked.

"No, I wouldn't," he said. We laughed.

I purchased one of the books, "The Further Sounding Doves," that I had been flipping through to add to my collection of books on poetry. I loved reading poems by poets who for the most part went unrecognized and under-appreciated. The cashier said that the Bible was old and that I could have it for free. I thought it would have been a collector's item for sure.

"It must have gotten mixed in with the books that were for sale," she said. "It's not really worth anything," she added, placing it carefully in the bag with the other books.

We crossed the street and walked down the block to Uno's on Sixth Avenue in the village and we had lunch. Over chicken thumbs and mozzarella garlic bread, I discovered that this man was gorgeous. He had a leather knapsack that I hadn't noticed at the bookstore and a brightness that was illuminating. When he was in the room, you knew he was there. He sat modestly enjoying his meal and the conversation we were having. But the last thing I was looking for right now was more heartbreak. Not that he had asked. But if he did, I knew what I would say. No. I would definitely say no.

Sometimes you can be so up in someone's face that you can't see the forest for the trees. Benji was desirable, very articulate and from his forwardness I would guess heterosexual too. Just my type. Benji and I talked more about poetry, and then we got into an in-depth spiritual discussion. Christianity. He believed that there was one truth, not many. He believed that people created other religions by omitting what they find undesirable about the true religion.

He said, "When you omit, pervert or take anything away from the true religion then it was no longer truth, it was a lie."

It was so incredible. A good-looking man and an intense conversation.

He wasn't claiming to be perfect, but he wasn't disregarding his teaching either. He was a Christian man and I guess he thought I needed to know that. He explained about having been miseducated by his peers. "Christ wasn't a white man's God. God was spirit. Spirit had no color. Labeling God white or black was just the flawed humans way of picturing and comprehending God," he said.

I don't ever remember a man voluntarily getting into an in-depth discussion about anything but sports or themselves. Surely a sexist statement, but for me, true. Usually we have to back them up into a corner to get a word out of them, but Benji was definitely not like that. I guess saying that was being a bit stereotypical, but, then, who's perfect? All I've learned is from what I've experienced. I would have loved to have known men like Benji. Though I can only remember one young man who was even remotely similar. He was in my congregation and Bible study group. We were both seventeen. I've forgotten his name. His family moved to South Carolina. I'd given him my address but he'd never written. I had been heartbroken at the time because I had lost a good friend, not to mention that he was cute.

I wished that I could be more like Benji seemed to be. I was totally enjoying this conversation. When I was deep in church and praying all the time, I thought I was invincible. And to some degree I was. That was before folks started telling me that I was "too deep." I could still never gather what they really meant by that though. Did they mean, worship God, but don't worship God? It was confusing to say the least. It was ironic that the same people who should teach you, could turn around and tear you down.

"You can't be so straightforward," and "You're too deep for me, girl," they would tell me. Or they would insinuate that "It was a shame that I always had to talk about God everywhere I went." What I needed most was a sister-friend who believed, since most people said that men and women couldn't be "just friends." But that was the last thing I found. I found myself alone a lot, since most of the church was coupled off, and I refused to be hopeful every time a single man joined the church. So, I lightened up, which didn't benefit me in the least. It went from an occasional glass of wine with dinner to cocktails at his place and Belgian waffles in the morning for breakfast. No sex, but a compromising situation nevertheless. With every summer I would slip further and further away from God. It seemed easier to let go when the weather changed.

My thoughts turned to fanciful things, and pleasure was in the forefront of my mind. The birds sang and the warm morning breeze blew; you didn't even need a jacket anymore. It was perfect handholding weather. An occasional car would cruise down the street at seven in the morning, and I'd watch the newspaperman on the corner. Everything bloomed, including my heart. Backsliding. It was the slowest decline into oblivion.

I watched those same people who told me I was too deep, and always told me that I didn't have to dress so frumpy or that I should let down my hair, fall away from God and the church. I soon followed, realizing that those whose opinions I valued the most, I should have valued the least. In the end it was the shame of being influenced so easily by the roaring lion that kept me away from my faith and the church. My life had been a slow, but camouflaged downward spiral.

How wonderful it must be to be totally dedicated to something and not have it dull your creativity. There were many people who thought that if you believed in God that you should have one pair of shoes and look as close to homeless as you possibly could to be considered humble. What incredible lies. Benji had exactly what I wanted. He possessed zeal, determination and a genuine love of God.

Benji and I talked about art too, and I mentioned that I had just started back painting, which was no big deal but he seemed to take a genuine interest in it and wanted to see what I could do. I didn't tell him that I started back painting after I went fool when I got stood up the other night, but he inquired about whether or not I was artistically inclined and I said, "Yes." It was true. He was what some might consider overly-curious though. Either he really loved art or he was trying desperately to get me back to my place. I figured he really loved art, since Benji didn't seem like the pushy one night stand type, but then again, who ever seemed like the type. They always came neatly disguised as something perfect.

I excused myself to call the house, I mean, it wasn't like I had anything else to do. I wanted to show this fine specimen of a man what I was capable of. Artistically speaking, that is. A creative black woman who looked good and was in great physical shape, ecetera, ecetera. Since I'm an artist, though I use that word loosely, maybe he would even model for me. I called to see if Joe was still at the apartment or if she had left already, but no one picked up. The machine came on. She would usually pick up if she was there, wouldn't she? I returned to the table and smiled.

"Okay, Benji, are you ready?"

"Sure," he said, as he motioned for the waitress and paid the check.

I was mumbling under my breath, "Please, God, don't let him be a maniac. Don't let him be a maniac."

Chapter Nine

I walked into my apartment, saying a silent prayer to myself that Joe had made the bed. The same bed with crumpled sheets that we had shared hours earlier. Opening the apartment door, I could smell the sweet fragrance wafting from the flowers in the vase. Joe was gone and she had made the bed. She had also left me a note that I put in my pocket to read later, and my machine was blinking two. The catastrophic creations that I had taken out all of my passion, lust, hate, revenge, and not to mention, anger out on, were propped up on the chairs. The light was beaming through the curtains and across the glass table, reflecting a rainbow on the ceiling.

"Very interesting," he said, looking at my work. "Don't take this the wrong way, Lea, but, with the sharp lines and dark hues, I see a lot of pain in your work."

"Really?" I nodded slowly. "I'm not offended. Actually, that's very perceptive of you," I said, pleased that I had met a man who was not only good-looking but could appreciate art.

I was shocked, unless a man had studied art he really didn't have much of an opinion or a clue.

"Your work is phenomenal, where did you study art?"

"No, it's just kind of a hobby and something I do when I'm bored, angry or trying to relax."

"You're very funny, and talented too," he added. I made coffee, and over mocha-something I asked him the usual where he was born, what did he do questions. He said he was born in Maryland, Benjamin Braithwait, but he was raised in New York City. He's thirty-three years old, born on January 2, reborn under a tent service about four summers ago, and he was a freelance writer who had published a couple of articles in various magazines about men, women and relationships.

He liked music. All kinds, not just R&B and gospel. His mother used to take him and his cousin to the ballet and the opera. He seemed to be very cultured and well-rounded. He had a genuine appreciation for music.

"I could never get the hang of country though," he said. I began to tell him about me and how I liked to write poetry and wanted to write a novel one day. He kept gazing into the paintings. He said he was working on something entitled, "The Fire Inside - Fear of Intimacy." He was explaining to me how if a man had a fear of intimacy, it smoldered inside of him until it became a fire. He thought people should express how they felt.

"The fire prevented anyone from getting close," he said. He was confident, for lack of a better adjective. He's definitely not a bum. But if my mother knew I had met this man less than three hours ago, and that he was now sitting on my sofa in my apartment, she would probably have had me committed. Never mind that I felt comfortable with him and that I thoroughly enjoyed his company; Moma would call the paddywagon.

He had a nice healthy head full of neatly divided dreadlocks. They weren't too thin or too thick. He had been growing them for ten years, he said. He wasn't caught up in what people thought of him, or the way he looked. He let me touch them. They were soft and moist. Not at all like I thought they would feel. He wasn't a dread or a Rasta; he was just Benji, he said. His locks had no spiritual significance, although the people who approached him on the street thought they did and were rather disturbed when he told them that they didn't. He liked the look so he had adopted it. It's so good to know that he wasn't following society's fashion trends. Fashion was an individual thing, I just wish more people realized that.

His nails were well-manicured and he was wearing Fahrenheit. It was intoxicating and now it was beginning to feel like I'd known him all my life. I inhaled slowly and he was sitting comfortably in my apartment and didn't seem at all as nervous as I remember some guys being. When we had organized a fellowship or potluck for the church, and the men happened to arrive before the women did, it was a tragic situation.

"Maybe I should go and come back," they'd say. Men should never be alone in a woman's apartment, and vice-versa. I never understood that, we were adults. But, maybe that was the point.

He was talking to me casually, and he was so relaxed that he would lean over and get close to my face without really noticing. I had the constant urge to kiss him, but I held my breath instead. I was watching his lips move, yet didn't hear a word he said sometimes. His hands were gesturing and telling a story. His lips were full and looked incredibly moist. I needed something to take my mind off of Mark, and it was working. Even now in the presence of Benjamin my memory of Mark was beginning to get a little fuzzy and it hadn't even been twenty-four hours yet.

Benji has beautiful dark brown skin and more than enough hair on his face to tell you he was a man. It made you just want to touch him to see if he was real. I wondered how he would kiss me. They say that you can tell how a man makes love by how he kisses you. I guess they meant that if he was really creative in the way he kissed, then that meant that he was a wonderful lover. Probably a myth, perhaps, but I couldn't help but wonder how soft his hands were and how he would touch me if I let him. I wondered where he would touch me? Peculiar little thoughts raced through my mind, as he seemed to woo me with his words. I knew he wouldn't kiss me. He was a respectable man, and I was thinking things I shouldn't, even though I was human. The flesh always gets you into trouble. I remembered that from discipleship class. Crucify it. Crucify the flesh.

There was nothing specific he said, it was sort of an aura. He was mentally and physically stimulating. Lunch was great, conversation was good, it was getting late, so we exchanged numbers, smiles and a hug, as I reluctantly walked him to the door. He complimented me on a sculpture that Rhonda had given me for my birthday a year or two ago. It was like an "All God's Children" figurine, but more expensive and with more intricate detail. It was a carving of a woman and a child by a black sculptor. Thomas Blackshear.

Benji was very very interesting, warm and confident. His dinner invitation for tomorrow night told me that he also found me intriguing and interesting too. I had to take it slow though. I was still nursing fresh wounds. Mark shot me through the heart and Sasha stabbed me in the back. I was a member of the "walking wounded," and my pain was my membership card. Although I wasn't going to let that ruin my date tomorrow night. I was excited.

I rushed to the window, hoping to get a look at him walking down the street. No Porsche, no Mercedes, and he's a writer, not a drug dealer. He's clean, soft spoken and God fearing. I had struck gold. My mind was reeling. He was

65

about 5'8 and he made Mark look like a rugrat, or something less appealing. A pitiful comparison, but true. I pulled out the note that Joe had left for me.

"I'm sorry about last night. Call me - Joe." There were two messages on my machine. When I played them back, one was Joe, who said she needed to talk to me, and the other was James who said he would be here at seven-thirty to pick up the paintings. I called Joe.

Joe understood my needs and didn't take it personally that last night just sort of happened. She was sorry that it actually went that far because she said she cared about what I felt. She apologized profusely. I know that Joe was a true friend and that she really did have my best interest at heart. Not like Sasha. Besides I wasn't all freaked out because I know that I'm not a lesbian. But now I know that I'm definitely not homophobic either. People don't turn gay. That was a horrible myth.

People are curious and people do experiment but they don't "turn" gay. I'm not going to be gay tomorrow because she touched me last night. I could ask myself why I responded the way I did to her but I wasn't up to self-analysis. Thoughts of Sasha and Mark began to flood my mind. I envisioned them together, caressing and sharing what he and I had never managed to. I couldn't help but think that to be on Benji's arm would be the best revenge. Not that I would use Benjamin, because I wouldn't. I valued him for what he was, someone I had just met and liked very much.

The doorbell rang. It was James, bearing flowers as usual, and the freak-of-the-week, Steve. What, are they joined at the hip? I thought.

"So, are you working on anything new?" James asked, as he strolled in looking around. Is he kidding? I thought.

"No," I smiled reluctantly. "I haven't really had the time."

"So how are you, Lea?" Steve asked, walking in like he lived here.

"I'm fine."

"Yes, you sure are," he said, "you sure are."
As the kids would say, don't even try it. There is no way this dog of a man was gonna get anywhere near this.

"These are for you," James said, presenting me with pink wilting carnations.

"Thanks, James. You really shouldn't have."

My mind wandered. I was totally taken by Benjamin. I couldn't help but think that tomorrow's headlines would read: "Woman falls head over heels for mystery man." I can't even articulate how purposely I would love Benji if I had the chance.

"So, James, when is the show?" I asked again, changing the subject in my mind.

"Wednesday at the Beekman. I'll let you know how it goes. I really have to jet," he said, as he covered the paintings with a paint-stained drop cloth that looked like a work of art itself, and they left me to my delicious thoughts.

I don't know what it was, but I couldn't shake Benji. He made a lasting impression on me. He was cool, calm and wasn't pawing all over me. He didn't even try to kiss me. Not that I would have minded, but I'd like to take it slow. It's good to be patient for a change. The man wasn't leaving on the midnight train to Georgia. Even though it's more than obvious to me that I'm physically and mentally attracted to him. I can wait, I thought, I can wait.

I decided to stop down the hall to see how Nia was feeling. I hoped she didn't feel like I brushed her off the other night. Even though I would have much rather shared with her than be tortured by the scene at Sasha's house. She was dressed in a navy and white striped pant set, and welcomed me in as if nothing had happened. She wore shades and hurried around the kitchen as if to avoid the fact that I had seen her looking quite battered not so many hours ago. "I'm making iced tea, would you like some?"

"Sure."

"So, Lea... how was your date Friday night?"

"Well, it wasn't," I said. "The little simpleton... I mean, I don't think it's going to work out with Mark. I was getting too hyped-up over nothing," I said.

"You mean it's over, girl?"

"Yeah, I had to cut him loose, move on."

"Really?"

"So, Nia...where's Freddie," I asked hesitantly. Trying to change the topic off of my saga of a life.

"He's at the gym," she said, quite matter-of-factly.

"So what did he say?" I asked, sitting next to her on her exquisite navy damask sofa, fiddling with the Limoges she has so methodically arranged on the marble and glass coffee table.

"He was drunk, Lea. I mean, I've been dating him for over a year now and this never happened before."

"So he assured you it would never happen again?" I responded sarcastically.

"He loves me, Lea."

"Have you told anybody else what happened?"

"There's no need to, I rescheduled all of my appointments for next week, I'll be fine by then."

The doorbell rang and a look of panic flashed across Nia's face.

"Do you want me to get it?" I asked.

"Would you?"

"Sure."

"Delivery for Ms. Nia Cole?" The short Mexican-looking fellow with a gray sweathood and a Yankee baseball cap handed me the flowers.

"I'll sign for it," Nia said, and reached out from behind me, folding up what looked like $5.00, and gave it to the delivery guy.

"Thank you," he murmured in heavily accented English and hurried off.

"They're beautiful, Nia," I said, looking at the orange-red tipped roses that were so fragrant and alive that they appeared to be almost ready to burst open.

"Open the card, girl! Open it!"

"You open it," she said, nonchalantly.

"Hoping these make you feel better, call me soon, Lance."

"Lance? Who's Lance, Nia?" I smiled teasingly.

"Lance is the friend who left a message on my machine. Lance is the reason I look like this, Lea."

I looked at the fading bruises on her cheekbone, and her lip that was beginning to heal.

"Nia, no one is to blame but Freddie. You can't blame this guy," I consoled. "He's innocent. The most he is guilty of is dialing 1-800-flowers to send you some."

She would rather blame a guy she wasn't interested in rather than face the truth that Freddie had a problem. A big problem. A problem that could leave her in an emergency room with tubes down her throat. I wanted to tell her all about my new friend, the guy who had my interest. The guy who was articulate, charming and had the most beautiful head full of locks that I had ever seen. But I didn't dare. Especially with what's going on in her life now. Just when you thought you had it bad, look at someone else's situation. Moma always said that.

69

Chapter Ten

I usually dreaded Monday mornings, but tonight I had a date so I was full of pep and vigor. I got up and took a nice long hot shower and put on my favorite perfume. I rummaged through my closet for something comfortable to wear today. Labels didn't seem to mean as much to me since I met Benji. I had more important things to daydream about lately than when **Donna Karan** was having her next sale. I couldn't live in a fantasy world of labels that gave you super power and made you feel that you ruled the world. The phone rang. It was Moma. She wanted to know if I had heard from Cheyenne. She says that she's hasn't been home or at work in three days. I assured Moma that she was okay wherever she was, although it wasn't at all like her to run off anywhere without calling. She said she had enough to worry about with Todd and the kids, but I told her that I'd call her if I heard anything and she assured me that she'd do the same.

I knocked on Craig's door to see if he could drop my carpet off at the cleaners for me first thing this morning. It had paint all over it and it looked like it had been postmarked in Mardi Gras. Craig came to the door, happier

70

to see me than he was to do the favor that I was asking. "I just hope the paint stains come out," I said, leaving the rolled carpet by his door.

"I'm sure they will," he said. Craig is my neighbor. He lives directly across the hall from me. He helps me out and runs a lot of errands for me when I don't have the time. He's on disability and I try to give him a few dollars whenever I can. You know, help a brother out. He was grateful and so was I.

Nicky says that she gets the impression that he has a thing for me and that he would probably do anything I asked for free, but that's not my problem. I'm not here to serve every hungry man on earth. They have soup kitchens for that. I have no problem paying for what I need done. Besides, there's nothing there. I don't feel anything when I look at him, and I definitely don't sit and daydream about the brother. No chemistry. No spark. Nevertheless he's helpful and dependable. I don't know what I would do without him, or Terry. I hoped I could get the carpet back tonight because my floors looked bare without it.

"Craig, can you tell them that the stains are acrylic paint?"

"Okay," he smiled, nodding his head up and down like he was moonstruck. I gave him some cash and left.

When I made it to work, Terry handed me three messages. Two messages were from Mark and one was from Benji. Benji said..."looking forward to seeing you tonight, will call you at home." I just wanted him to breathe on me, to touch me or something. Right here, right now. He had such a caring nature and sweet disposition, I could sense that already. He made me feel alive. Unlike Mark who made me feel twice dead and plucked up by the root.

I wondered what Mark was doing now. Probably thinking of something he could buy me to get me to forgive him. Some things just can't be forgiven though. I know

I should still be on guard after all the drama Saturday night, but I just can't seem to be that way with Benji. I called Joe. She was my advocate. I left a message on her voicemail and asked her if she could call Mark and tell him that I didn't want to talk to him and he should stop calling me at work. We were all friends. She's talked to him about various things, so I'd doubt she'd mind talking to him about this. I also said that if he wanted to know why I changed my number, tell him that he's not worth the breath that it would take to explain it to him.

Meeting after pencil tapping meeting, today was the longest day of my life. It reminded me of the last day of school when I was a kid. I thought the day would never end so that summer vacation could officially begin. Looseleaf books, paper and pencils went flying in the air the minute the school bell rang, although I couldn't do that here. I counted the seconds as they ticked away closer to 5:00 P.M.

"Lea, would you like to go out and get some coffee, cappuccino, or something after work?"

"Oh, William, I can't, I'm busy tonight." Although William was tall and handsome, he was just not my type. He was my business associate; we had at least six projects that we were working on together. His interest in me was obvious, but he was...well, to put it nicely, boring. But I guess when you were totally into someone like I was with Mark, everyone else paled by comparison.

"Maybe tomorrow William," I said, knowing good and well tomorrow would never come. The look on his face was disappointment, but who was I to go around distributing satisfaction?

"Goodnight, Terry," I said on my way out as I hurried home to wash and blow out my hair. I thought over in my mind what I would wear. I put on a simple black dress, no longer because black was Mark's favorite color, but because I looked good in black. Everyone did. I adorned myself with simple pieces of silver jewelry and only a spritz of Day from the Gap. The telephone rang and I got a chill. I knew it was Benji. I could feel it. Have you ever felt a man breathing on the phone before you even picked it up? It was like racing down the highway doing ninety-five. It gave me a tingle. I was gasping to catch my breath. I let the phone ring one more time, so as not to seem too anxious.

I would love to put all of the passion and feeling that I used to put into Mark, into Benji now. Benji deserved it, Mark never did. I was attempting to heal myself. Even though it would be different because what Mark and I had was imaginary, and what Benji and I are developing into is real. I could fall in love with Benji, which wouldn't be hard or so far fetched.

"Hello?" Benji sounded delicious over the telephone. He said he'd be here at eight. At seven-thirty the intercom buzzed and I was amazed that the man was not only on time but early.

I opened the door with anticipation, and to my dismay it was Mark. I tried to close the door in his face, but he forced his way in. He stood there with his saddened eyes looking at me like he was the one who had been hurt. His dark close-cut hair and thick eyebrows scrunched in a pitiful frown. His silk shirt with the first few buttons undone was such a feeble attempt to distract. I'd just die I thought if he was still here when Benji came. The last thing I needed Benji to think was that I was playing some kind of game.

"Did you get my messages?" he said, barely above a whisper.

"Did you get mine!" I snapped. Mark told me he had something to tell me and he didn't know how I would take it. He said that he cared about me a lot and didn't want to hurt me. He said he loved me but. Here it comes, I thought. But he said that he loved Sasha and that he was going to marry her. He said that he loved me, too, but he was confused. He went on and on about how he never meant to hurt me and how he was sorry about the rings, Friday night and everything. He said that Sasha needed to see him Friday night, so he had to cancel our date. That's when he got the news that she was pregnant.

He also said that she wanted to tell me first, before I found out some other way. I didn't believe for a second that Sasha waited until her fourth month to tell him she was pregnant. He was full of it! I thought I was near death. It felt like I was being asphyxiated. Suffocated not only by his presence but his lies. Why is it that when people say that they never meant to hurt you, that you still end up hurting anyway and they end up doing exactly what they know that they wanted to do from day one? Did they think that by saying that they never meant to hurt you that it would console you? It didn't. I asked him to leave. He wanted to explain. Explain what? How he loved two women equally? How he wanted us both? How I should feel flattered that he will never forget me? I don't want to be somebody's memory; I want to be someone's future.

He said he was sorry. I told him that I would get someone to make him leave. That's when the doorbell rang. It was Benji, I just knew it. I felt him. Tears began to stream down my cheeks. Not only did I lose Mark, but I was about to lose what hadn't even begun with Benji, because Mark was here at my place and it would appear to be more than it actually was. I opened the door, and I was literally a mess. My eyeliner had begun to run and so had my nose.

"Lea? Are you okay? What's going on?"

"He was just leaving, Benji."

"No, I wasn't, I just got here!"

"Mark, you have to go!" I cried.

"I'm not done, Lea. I came here to iron all this out."

"Man, just leave. She wants you to leave," Benji said.

"Who are you?" Mark asked.

"This is between me and Lea. I'm not leaving until I'm done."

I ran to the bathroom and locked the door.

"Are you satisfied, man?" Benji asked.

"I don't need this," Mark stormed off, and slammed the door on his way out.

"Are you alright?" Benji consoled through the bathroom door.

"I'm fine," I said.

"Can I talk to you, Lea?"

"I guess so," I said, opening the door. He held out his hands and I took them. He was holding me in those strong arms of his. As he held me, I felt protected and confident that I no longer needed Mark. Not because of Benji, but because I finally said no to Mark and didn't give in. He had officially dumped me, yes, but I didn't go begging him to take me back. I wasn't begging him to let us just be friends in an attempt to make room for more.

"I'd never let anyone hurt you, Lea," Benji said. It sounded just like a movie. I believed him and I trusted him. I mean, so far so good, right?

Benji had been there for me. He was considerate and protecting. He was fantasy-like and I liked to think of him as my knight in shining armor. He rushed in right at the nick of time and released me from Mark's clutches. Mark who had sunk his claws in and tried to devour me. Mark had lured me to his cave with the bait and promise of more than a friendship, and I had bitten because I wanted nothing more in life than to care about somebody who had a job and was about something more than just sex.

I began to open up to Benji a little. If this was to have even a remote possibility of developing into anything at all, I would have to confess. Loose my demons.

"I loved Mark," I said. "I loved him and he's marrying one of my best friends. She's pregnant, and I bought him a ring because I was going to propose Friday night at dinner, but now everything is ruined," I rambled on. "My life is a mess."

"Shhh," he said. "Don't talk. Let's forget about everything. You deserve to be happy, girl. You are a wonderful woman."

He dried my tears and looked into my eyes and said, "You're still beautiful."

"Even with a runny nose?" I said, sniffling.

"Yes," he said, "even with a runny nose."

It wasn't hard opening up to Benji. He was easy-going and a good listener. He was the type of man who seemed to want to take care of a woman. I knew I was getting ahead of myself, but I couldn't help seeing that Benji could fit more perfectly into my life than Mark had.

"Let's get out of here," he said. We got into his car. It didn't matter what he drove. I was more impressed that he was gentle and understanding. I wasn't impressed by an Acura, Integra or Legend, it didn't matter. He could have been driving a Toyota get-out-and-push, and I would still feel what I was feeling now. Material things couldn't compare to happiness. The words lingered in the air. I couldn't believe that "I" was saying this. Not me, Miss Neiman Marcus. But it's all becoming so clear now. Material possessions didn't bring you happiness. Sure they filled the void for a short while, but you could be sitting at home in the middle of your floor with bags from Gucci, Tocoshymiya and Lord and Taylor but if you didn't have someone to console you, need you, or share with you, then what good were tangible things?

I know that I sounded like Buddha on the mountaintop, or Moses, Noah or someone from the Bible. But I felt changed. In that instant I knew that there were

LINDA DOMINIQUE GROSVENOR

things that I would have to overcome, and with the help of God and Benji, I could. As long as I believe, good things can happen. From what I remember, we are predestined. That means, God has a plan. I'm praying that Benji is in the plan God has for me. Although, now that I'm living my life without a hint of spirituality, it boils down to the fact that I am merely existing. No purpose, just here taking up space. I was like others who knew Him by name but never by face. But still I had to believe that Benji was part of that plan. I had to believe in God.

He had CeCe Winans, Maxwell, and a collection of other CDs. He told me to play what I liked.

"I love Maxwell," I said.

"Yeah, he's smooth."

Whitney was singing a song on the radio about how you could have diamonds in your hands and the riches of the land, but without love you don't really have nothing at all. She was right and I was beginning to see where I had gone wrong in my life. I had put so much importance on looks, labels and status, yet I was alone. Until now. This thing between Benji and I was possible, I believed that. I needed to believe it.

We put on Maxwell, and I was leaning back in my seat as we drove for what seemed like forever until we ended up at the quaintest little Italian restaurant in Connecticut. We were the only black couple in the restaurant, but the food was great and it felt like home. There were red and white checkered tablecloths on the tables, and a small candle flickering in a red votive, an Italian scenic mural made the walls of the restaurant look as if we were in Venice. We ate, and I talked. He listened and listened and listened. I liked that. Someone who actually wanted to hear what I had to say. Someone who thought that my feelings were important.

He never questioned me about Mark or the incident. He wasn't insecure. He was a man. Not the kind of man who had to puff up his chest and carry on to prove it. He was low key and gentle, but still a man. We enjoyed dessert and cappuccino and he assured me, it was okay. Everything would be fine. We drove home with the sunroof open and he pulled over to somewhere that was very secluded so that I could gaze at the stars. I loved the stars. It was magical. I felt like a princess. He was my king.

We had a lovely evening. Flowers, a glass of wine, dinner and a doggie bag. It had to be about two in the morning when we got back to the city. It didn't matter that I had to go to work in less than five hours either. Tonight was perfect, I thought. Well, almost perfect.

"Has anyone ever told you how beautiful you are?" he asked.

Before I could answer, his lips were drawing near. They were moist, sweet and melting me down on the inside. Now tonight *was* perfect.

"I want to rescue you, I want to protect you," he said. He was so close that I could taste his breath. "Will you let me?" he asked. He touched me and I was trembling. I was scared at what I could feel, what I was feeling right now. I had dreamt of perfection over and over again in my mind, and Mark had always been the center of my affection, but it was always make-believe. And it was always only in my mind. This was real. I didn't want tonight to be over but if I didn't end this, we might be in a situation that I'm not even sure that I could handle. Or even more than that.

"I have to go, Benji."

"Do you?"

"Yes, Benji."

"Will I see you tomorrow?"

"Do you want to?"

"Of course I do."

78

"Okay, you will," I grinned. He kissed me goodbye, and kind of brushed his lips against my cheek as I turned to go into my complex.

As soon as I stepped off the elevator and reached for my keys and put them in the apartment door, the phone was ringing. I hurried, inserting the keys to open the door, and ran to pick up before the answering machine did. It was Benji.

"Baby," he said, "I just wanted to say goodnight."

"Do you miss me yet?" I asked.

"Yes."

"So say it then."

"I miss you, Lea."

"Goodnight, Benji," I said in the sweetest voice I could conjure. I placed the receiver in the cradle and screamed out loud like I always do when feelings are so intense that I cannot contain them. He made me smile. He gave me something to look forward to. I couldn't wait to tell all of my friends. A love reciprocated, what a glorious feeling.

The phone rang again, and I smiled to myself thinking that maybe we'd talk all night.

"She moved out."

"Who moved out, Moma?"

"Cheyenne."

"Cheyenne moved out?"

"Yes, she moved back to New York."

"For what?"

"She lost her job and wanted to move back," she said. "She said she's looking for something in her field."

"She's a secretary, Moma, she doesn't have a field."

"I'm only telling you what she told me."

"Why did she lose her job?"

"I don't know, child, don't start me to lying. But, I guess it was from being out sick all the time and being late. The girl was out more than she was at work."

"How do you know, Moma?"

"I went to pick up her check at the office like she asked me to, and they told me."

"They just came right out and told you?"

"No, well, they pulled me to the side, Lea. But they said that the girl needs help. Always late, always nodding off at the computer, and always taking long lunches and sometimes never coming back. She's not professional at all, they said. Find your sister, baby, she's lost her mind."

She was chasing it. That's what her girlfriend Shondra said when I called her. Shondra worked at her job, too. That's where they had met. I called her up to see if she had heard from Cheyenne.

"We stopped hanging out months ago, Lea. She always wanted to try something new. I don't smoke. I don't even smoke cigarettes.

"She was always locked in my bathroom when she came over here. I told her she needed help and she told me to mind my business. So I did. My business is my daughter and she comes first. She comes before anybody. I gave up that life, Lea."

Shondra compared Cheyenne to a child spinning until she was dizzy to get that Jimmy Hendrix psychedelic high. She had to have about a $50-a-day crack habit. She was semi-functional, so no one really had a clue.

"She was always borrowing money from me, Lea. At work, alot of the deposits that the customers gave her for their insurance policies weren't turned in. The policies weren't initiated. They were calling and complaining that they hadn't received their policies."

Rumor had it that she was living on 116th Street with a friend, in this green building that was known for crack parties and orgies, and the likes of which would make any decent person cringe. I walked down the street and could hear the music before I even walked through the front door of the building. It was the only building on the block that wasn't boarded up. I made my way past people who were waving their pipes and combing the floors for something to put in it.

I never thought I'd see this life. Never! And especially not for my sister. Apartment 3C was hers and that's exactly where the music was coming from. There were strobe lights and lava lamps in all different colors in the four corners of the room. I thought I was having a 70's flashback. I walked in and no one said a word. They all looked up just long enough to see if I was passing them something to smoke, and then went back to their routine. I looked around and there was a dim light on in the kitchen. There were dishes in the sink with green hairy stuff growing on them, and newspapers were strewn all over the floor. This couldn't be where Cheyenne lived, I thought. Not my classy sister. But it was apartment 3C. I couldn't find her.

People were pawing each other. The stench of stale weed was throughout the house. It was stronger in certain places than others. Somebody was in the corner sniffing what could have been either cocaine or heroine off of a broken piece of mirror. The furniture was old and looked like it must have been left from the people who lived there ten years ago. I pushed my way into the bedroom and there had to be about five people naked on the bed doing God knows what. They were moving in slow motion, and there were all sorts of colors and velvet zodiac pictures on the walls, it smelled awful.

I closed the door and nudged my way into the bathroom and there was Cheyenne. She was kneeling down on the filthy floor pleasing a man I'm sure she hardly knew.

The tub was backed up and smelled of rancid water, as did the toilet that had three rings of color around the inside of the bowl.

"Let's go, Cheyenne!"

"Hey, Lee."

"Let's go, Cheyenne!"

"Go where, Lee? I'm having a party," she said in her slurred speech.

"No, girl, the party is having you! Let's go!"

"I'm not leaving my guests!"

"Girl, this is hardly a dinner party. Get up!"

"C'mon, baby," the guy said, in a slow drawled high. "She's not done yet."

"Oh, she's done—trust me!" I grabbed her by the wrist, just like Moma used to do when we were bad and she couldn't wait to get us home. I dragged her through the crowd and didn't stop until we were downstairs. I pulled her behind me and then shoved her into the rent-a-car.

"What are you looking at!" I yelled at a few curious on-lookers, who seemed more interested in the parts to my car than what I was actually doing to Cheyenne.

She sat there, spacy as the Twilight Zone. This girl was roasted, toasted and burnt to a crisp.

"A quickie in the bathroom, Cheyenne?"

"Either it was an earthquake or he was rocking my world," she said, laughing.

"Cheyenne, you need help, girl. Moma said you just moved out. Why did you leave Moma there all by herself?"

"I'm not my Moma's keeper," she said. My better judgment wasn't functioning, so I slapped her so hard, her face hit the passenger side window. She laughed, as if she didn't feel a thing. Crack will do that to you, I guess. Like all drugs, they numbed the senses.

I called Moma the minute I got in. It had to be about 5:00 A.M. here so it was probably 4:00 A.M. there.

"Moma, I found her."

"What was she doing?"

"You'd never want to know that. Never! I'll call you back, Moma."

I called Nicky. "Wake up! Wake up! Wake up!"

"Hello?"

"Nicky, come over here right now!"

"For what? It's 5:00 A.M., Lea," she groaned.

"Your sister is here and she's doing bad."

"Who? Cheyenne?"

"Yes, Cheyenne."

"Bad how?"

"I'm not going to talk about this on the phone, Nicky."

"Okay, okay. I'm coming."

I paged Benji since I honestly didn't have anyone else to call. In a situation like this I would have easily called Mark, but not now.

"What's up," Nick said, when she arrived dressed in pajamas and a trench coat.

"Your sister was on 116th street getting high in a crack house" I explained while fighting back tears.

"What?"

"Yes, I had to pull her out of there."

"Moma said she moved out."

"She left Moma there, Lee?"

"Yes. Moma was worried to death. She has a problem Nick."

"So, what do we do?"

"I don't know. I called Benji."

"Who?"

"Benji, he's a friend."

The phone rang almost immediately.

"Lea? Are you alright?"

"Benji? I can hardly hear you."

"I'm on the cell phone, what's wrong Lea?"

"I have a little emergency here Benji and I didn't know who else to call."

"Slow down. What's wrong?"

"I can't say over the phone Benji. I didn't know who else to call."

"Okay, okay, I'll be there soon. Less than forty-five minutes, okay?"

"Okay."

Cheyenne was staring out of the window and saying that she didn't know what all the fuss was about.

"Y'all trippin. I'm fine," she assured.

"You're so fine that you had your mother worried to death."

"She'll be fine, Lee. Moma will be fine," Cheyenne said.

"You're so stupid, Cheyenne. I never expected this out of you. Drugs? You know Moma has a weak heart."

Nicky looked wide-eyed and shook her head in disbelief. "You're going back, Chey!"

"I'm not going anywhere!"

"Oh, yes you are! You will get back on the plane and find another job and make sure Moma can pay her bills like you've been doing."

"Moma's not my responsibility, Lea."

"Shut up Chey! Just shut up!"

The phone rang again. It was Moma.

"Put Cheyenne on the phone, will you, Lea."

I tossed the phone at Cheyenne. I was more upset than I've probably ever been in my life.

"Yes, Moma," Cheyenne said, lowering her tone a bit.

"Are you alright?"

"I'm fine, Moma."

"Your boss called here."

"For what, to fire me again?" she laughed.

"He said that they want to bring you up on criminal charges for the money you stole, Cheyenne. It's a federal offense."

"What money Moma?"

"You still lying, huh? Cheyenne they have signed contracts where the customers signed applications to initiate life insurance policies. You took the money, didn't you, Cheyenne?"

"What money, Moma? I don't know what you're talking about."

"Enough! Stop lying, child. Don't you know when you're deep enough?"

Cheyenne began to cry.

"I can't go to jail, Moma. I can't."

"If you go into a program, Cheyenne, he said they won't touch you."

"A program?"

"A drug program."

"I don't need a program, Moma."

"You need something, girl, and if you don't get help you go to jail."

Cheyenne handed me the phone. Moma told me what happened. She wanted to know who would fly back with her. Nicky said she would. She said she'd call her professors from there and let them know she had a family emergency.

Benji arrived just as I was on the phone trying to get tickets for Nicky and Chey to fly back down to Florida. "I'm not staying, Lee," Nicky said. "I'm just dropping her off and that's it."

"That's fine, Nick," I said.

"What's going on, Lea?" Benji asked. "My sister. She's mixed up in drugs and stuff like that. She left my mom in Florida and came here to New York. She had an apartment on 116th Street and...and."

"It's okay, Lea," he consoled with his hand on my shoulder.

"Benji, this is my sister Nicky, and that over there is Cheyenne."

"Nice to meet you," he said. Nicky smiled and nodded.

Benji drove us to the airport and we waited what seemed like hours until the flight was ready for boarding. Nicky was the youngest and it seemed like she was taking charge. I phoned the office and told Terry that I had an emergency. She said that she would let Mr. Emerson know. Cheyenne and Nicky were off to the side talking and I leaned over to Benji and asked, "Has my charm worn off yet?"

"C'mon, Lea, this is no reflection on you. We all have our flaws." I wanted someone who loved me, flaws and all, I thought to myself. He kissed my forehead and held my hand. He assured me that he found me just as attractive after being up all day and night as he did the moment he saw me.

I gave Nicky some money, but refused to give Cheyenne a dime.

"Call me the minute you get there, Nicky."

"Okay," she promised.

"Nice meeting you, Benji."

"Likewise," he said.

Cheyenne didn't say a word, and that was fine by me. We drove back to the city in perpetual silence. I didn't know what to say or how to say it. So I didn't.

Benji was making breakfast while I called Joe to fill her in on what had been going on. She's okay, I assured. "Nicky flew back with her."

"Where's the syrup Lea?" I had no appetite but I enjoyed his company nonetheless. We talked about second chances and I assured him that after awhile I would come around to Cheyenne. It was more anger than anything else. I was disappointed in her. Nicky was wild and might be prone to behavior like this but never in a million would I think this of Cheyenne.

"If you'd like we could go for a drive later, or just talk, if you want to," Benji said. His words were strong and comforting.

"I'd like that."

"How about seven?"

"Okay."

"Get some rest and I'll talk to you soon," he said kissing me on my forehead.

I called Nia to see how things were; she assured me things were fine. She and Freddie were still going at it hot and heavy. I told her about Cheyenne to sort of change the subject. I wanted her to feel at ease, not like I was judging her. I was her friend, and I wanted her to know that. The last time I stopped by she had all of her teeth, and her bruises were healing, but there was still something different. She didn't speak with the same enthusiasm anymore, not about her job or about life.

"I'm sorry about your sister," she said, though I didn't want to re-live that whole ordeal. I was sad that I couldn't tell Nia I had met someone. Someone beautiful, creative, well versed and strong. She was my friend but I didn't want to cover her with my gushing and praise, going on and on about how wonderful Benji was. Her doorbell rang.

"I have to go, Lea," she said before she hung up and the line went dead.

Benji and I drove up to the Bronx to Pelham. Glenn Island Park. We watched the ducks and swans swim in unison. There were men fishing in the dusk. They stood in the water with boots knee-high; they had nets and pails to put their catch in. The sun was almost gone. The birds talked back to each other and I could smell the fresh cut grass. The reminder of today's events were fresh in my head though. I kept envisioning Cheyenne on her knees. Benji broke the tension. He asked me what I thought I'd be when I grew up. I smiled. I'd been doing a lot of that lately.

"As a little girl, I always thought I'd be a stewardess and a ballerina."

"I thought I'd be a writer," he said. How true to life his childhood dreams were. Some of us had more realistic goals than others.

Benji held my hand and told me that it would be alright. He put his arms around me and thanked me for calling him.

"I'd usually have called Mark, you know, but since...you know."

"I know. Call me anytime," he smiled. His lips spoke truth. I needed a little of that in my life now. Truth. We drove back downtown and stopped for ice-cream on the way.

"What's your favorite flavor?"

"Pralines and Cream. Lots of sprinkles."

"How much is a lot?" He smiled.

"A cup full."

"Oh, so you want sprinkles with a little bit of ice-cream, huh?"

We laughed, for the first time all evening. I was comforted as he laughed with me.

"You are so special, Lea," Benji said as he held me close.

"Very special."

And I was happy. "You say the kindest things, Benji." He parted his lips and kissed me.

There was a perfection that hung in the air. Like a cool summer night that you never wanted to end. Just like when we drove to Connecticut. The non-verbal way that he was telling me that he'd be there for me. Not just tonight, but for a long while, and what would hopefully turn into forever. We smiled at each other and silence was a good thing now. I was making the transition from dull, draining relationships to meaningful, reciprocal commitment. Womanhood.

As we neared my complex, I sighed, not wanting to leave him. Not wanting him to go. It seems I never wanted a second I spent with Benji to end, but it was that second that transpired and allowed the next. I could accept that. Blackstreet was singing, "Let's Stay Together" and for the first time since I've heard the song, it finally applied to a part of my life. I could relate to staying together, in love and devoted.

Benji brushed my hair out of my eyes and face. "I just want to look at you," he said. I smiled, not too much, not too little. He was playing with my hair, running his fingers through it and twirling it a bit, just like Josai had done not so many days ago. He held onto me with his eyes.

"I...I...think I should go, Benji." I wasn't sure I could handle the feelings that were whirling through me at this very second, but I was convinced that I'd try, just not right now.

I knew that although he was affectionate I could not ask him to abandon all that he had been taught and everything that he believed in to comfort me. I needed to make decisions of my own. I needed to find a strength that would help me through these trying times. I needed what they called "a double portion." I needed God.

89

Chapter Eleven

First thing in the morning, Craig was ringing my bell.

"I tried to return your carpet but you weren't home," he said. I was standing there, smiling like a sixteen-year old.

"Are you okay," Craig said. I wondered if he could tell that I was blushing. I was as content as the cat that swallowed the canary, and as giddy as a schoolgirl who had just been asked out by the cutest guy in the school.

"I tried to call you too and leave a message, but your number is changed."

"I know, Craig. Thank you."

He stood there with a puzzled look on his face, scratching his head.

"I've gotta run, Craig, I'm going to be late for work. Thanks for taking the carpet for me."

"Okay, Lea, have a nice day."

"You, too, Craig." He stood there looking in as I closed the door. I never knew what to truly make of Craig.

I was doing that floating on a cloud thing. There was a time when I didn't do clouds. Cloud nine they called it, though I don't know why. I dawdled my way through work today and whenever the phone rang I got butterflies in my stomach. I checked my machine from the office about six times. Zero messages. Moma called to tell me that Cheyenne had arrived safely and that Nicky was on her way back. Shondra agreed to help Moma out while Cheyenne was in rehab. I was truly grateful for that. Shondra was more of a friend than Cheyenne could imagine.

Cheyenne's boss agreed to drop the charges.

"She was a great worker, she probably just got mixed up with the wrong crowd," he said. Not many people were given a second chance. My day couldn't end soon enough. I didn't get an ounce of work done; my boss was in San Fernando. William had a meeting with one of the clients from his solo account at 4:30, and it was a quarter to four. Terry brought me lunch back when she went out but I couldn't eat it. Love, adoration, intense emotion, or whatever the politically-correct expression for the 90's was, had totally destroyed my appetite.

William helped himself to my lunch as we wrapped up the designs for the Newell Project, and I daydreamed through most of his ideas. What was this thing? I couldn't even think straight.

Terry buzzed me. "Someone's here to see you, Lea."

Startled by the buzzer I spilled my coffee all over transmitted faxes and proposals. William buzzed her back, "Well, who is it, Terry?"

She usually announces everyone. Benji emerged into my office bearing what had to be almost three dozen lavender roses. I was amazed and blushing, though I didn't know which took precedent. I felt the blood rush to my face as I sat wearing a mixture of embarrassment and surprise, while still making an attempt to sop up the coffee and salvage the faxes. Terry was standing behind Benji, giving me the thumbs up sign. Spontaneity is his thing and I liked it.

"These are for you, Ms. Barnwell," he smiled, looking at my desk plate.

"William, this is Benjamin. Benjamin this is William, my colleague. We were working on some designs, but we're finishing up here."

William looked agitated, shook Benji's hand somewhat reluctantly, mumbled something under his breath and closed the door behind him as he left. Benji presented me the array of flowers and kissed me slowly and gently on my lips. All eyes were on me and my flowers as we left the office building. The guys that hung around the front desk of the accounts receivable department eyed me and checked out Benji. They were making a feeble attempt to discern how worthy he was to have me. I didn't know that men did that, or at least I thought they did it more discreetly.

A man with a sense of humor, I thought, as we joked and kidded through dinner at a little outdoor cafe in the village. He really makes me laugh. He's handsome, romantic, gentle and a definite possibility where love is concerned. One thing for sure, Benji kept me fed.

"Have you ever been to the Hot Pot?"

"Where?"

"The Hot Pot. It's a Jamaican restaurant."

"No, where is it?"

"In Harlem on Seventh Avenue, we must go there one evening, the food is excellent."

The mood was calm and I enjoyed driving up Madison Avenue, listening to AZ-Yet and looking at all the shops from the passenger window. After another lovely dining experience we were back on 96th Street and he graciously offered to walk me back to my apartment. I couldn't help but invite him in for coffee, cappuccino, latte or whatever else he had a taste for. My emotions were consuming me.

We sat on my red leather sofa, chatting. I didn't know that I could smile so much.

"Lea, I need to tell you something," he interrupted.

"You can tell me anything," I said, creating an atmosphere that was comfortable and familiar.

"What is it, Benji?"

"I think I'm falling in love with you."

There was a long pause that lasted almost a full minute.

"You think?" I said, trying to be as calm as possible as fireworks went off in my heart and I was rejoicing in my head that he had said it first.

"I know it hasn't been long but I've totally fallen, Lea."

"Totally?" I said shyly. He smiled. It was incredible that he was feeling the same thing that I was.

I wasn't a spring chicken, and at this point in my life I need someone who can be part of my future. I don't have time for merely dating for the sake of dating. I needed someone in my life that would stay put and would lead to something more than just casual sex.

Most of the time when you loved someone they didn't love you back, or when they love you you don't love them back, or as much. But here we both are feeling the same thing at the same time.

"Lea, I have to tell you something else," he said, as I'm thinking, could it get any better?

"I'm all ears," I smiled, decorating his face with sienna kisses.

"I don't know how to say it, Lea."

"Just say it, Benji. How bad can it be?"

"I'm married," he blurted out.

"Married?" My heart began to pound like I had run a ten-mile marathon. When it stopped pounding, I felt like it had been tossed off the tallest building in the city.

"Well, I guess you can say it's borderline divorce, but, yes, I'm married," he continued hesitantly. Borderline divorce? Talk about crash and burn. I went down in flames. It was an almost tragic situation. My mouth hung open and I could feel my heart crystallize.

Here was a man, seemingly dedicated to his faith, who had courted and comforted me for the past few weeks, and now he's telling me that he is married? I'm sure he'd have some logical explanation about how and why he had come on to me so deliberately, slowly but strongly. Maybe he'd explain why he couldn't help but tell me how beautiful I was every chance he got.

"My wife and I have been growing apart for years," he said, sounding slightly reminiscent of a soap saga. I smiled, but inside I was yelling and screaming why me, why me, trying to ignore that little voice that was saying, "I told you so." The whole atmosphere had changed. The expression on my face was disgust. However, I was cordial, I even hugged him in true friendship fashion. He wasn't going to see me sweat and I wasn't in the mood to hear his six-year saga of marital hell.

Married men were too much trouble, unless you were looking for some kind of game to play, and a married Christian man was definitely going back to his wife after the affair, it was inevitable and Biblical. He looked at me and said, he was sorry. Everyone's sorry. Mark's sorry, Benji's sorry and I'm sorry that I let it happen, I told myself.

He said he wasn't trying to run some kind of game but that he was just trying to be honest. We hugged and I wished to myself that this was a single man holding me in these strong arms. He looked into my eyes and whispered,

"I never lied to you, I do love you, Lea. I've loved you from the moment we met." What he said, caught me off guard.

How could he tell me that he was falling for me when he was committed to someone else? I didn't have the energy to fight for a man. No man was worth fighting over, I don't care how soft his lips were or how articulately he wooed me. He was absolutely off limits. I wasn't about to go there with him or his wife.

"Did you hear me, Lea? I said I love you?"

I lowered my eyes and took a deep breath that was somewhat exaggerated.

I looked up into his eyes. "How do you know, Benji?" I cooed. My tone was calm and subdued, even sensuous. My response alone made it all too clear that I had already been bitten. The love bug had sunk his teeth into my flesh and begun to feed on what had once been my protected heart.

"I think about you all the time, Lea. I miss you when I'm not here. I want to do things with you, to you and for you." I smiled and my lips quivered as his came near.

He kissed me gently and tenderly, and his arms held me so close it felt like we were one. I felt his heart beating through my chest and just when it felt like we were as close as we could get, he ran his fingers through the back of my hair, caressed my neck and pulled me even closer. Images of giving myself to this man flashed through my mind as he unbuttoned my blouse and turned me around slowly, slipping my blouse off, and kissing me on my shoulders and down the small of my back. Everything was slow and careful, but I didn't miss a thing.

I felt his hands glide across my body, they were strong yet soft. His touch was driving me wild. A kiss was a kiss, but a touch was worth a thousand words. It was so intense yet felt sufficient. I tried, but I couldn't resist. I tried to endure as much of his pleasure as I could, but I didn't know at what point to let him stop. I wasn't thinking,

I couldn't think. I was completely lost in the moment. Consumed, overtaken, caught up, overwhelmed. Pick an adjective and I was feeling it. I liked it. Matter of fact, I loved it. He was tender, I thought, as he lifted me up and carried me to the bedroom, where dimmed lights and Maxwell serenaded us with Whenever, Wherever, Whatever.

I was willing. I wasn't afraid. I've envisioned making slow deliberate love in my mind thousands of times, and now here I was running my fingers through his dreads and pulling him down on top of me in a gorgeous delicate moment. I wasn't at my desk, I wasn't in the bathtub and I wasn't watching '**Red Shoe Diaries.**'

"I love you, Lea."

"I love you, too. But Benji, I never..."

"Shhhhh..." he said as he put his soft warm lips on mine. He kissed his way down to my bellybutton and slipped my lace thong down over my hips. His strong warm hands roamed all over my moistened skin, stopping in places that I had once become all too familiar with.

My hormones told me, "Girl, this is it, abandon the S.S. Virgin and climb aboard the Love Boat." I thought how beautiful it was that I was here with this charming man who made words dance on his tongue. Allowing myself to give my heart and soul to another man would serve Mark right. He didn't deserve me. He couldn't handle me. He wasn't ready. He was still a child, Benji was a man.

Screams of passion escaped us, and the moans of delight that he shared gently in my ear, excited me to the point of bliss. It was slow, gentle and steady. He loved me so powerfully that I didn't see rainbows but there were literally bombs bursting in air. His locks brushed gently across my body, I was his. Totally and completely. He knew. He could see the look of pleasure on my face. Without me having to say it he knew. Softly he caressed me as though our love was enough. Enough for us, enough to create world peace, enough to satisfy me for a lifetime.

It was warm and our bodies were intertwined and intermingled. There was heat, there was passion and there was love. There were things I was feeling that I couldn't even articulate. My legs began to tremble as he held them tightly, and I was reciting beautiful poetry in my head.

"Your eyes were poetically suggestive, as they incited my virginal dance - cautiously I drank from you, becoming all too unsure of my fate."

"Tell me you want me, Lea," he breathed.

"I do, I want you," was all I could manage. And though I had become unsure of what we were sharing, my legs hugged him and his kisses felt like silk on my body, and I enjoyed him still.

I wished that I could make more of me for him to take. I wished that I had more of me to give him. There was a longing now. I was breathless with pleasure as he excited me. The gentle nudging and satisfaction of giving all that I had to this man was comforting. A man that I adored. I had arrived at the point where I could never find solace in being alone again. Never. Especially without Benji.

Maxwell was crooning "'Til the Cops Come Knockin'" and Benji held me and stroked my hair, beautifully and softly, kissed my glistening shoulders and the nape of my neck. The combination rocked me to sleep as he whispered something in my ear about love and wanting to be with me forever.

97

Chapter Twelve

I woke to the scent of him all over my pillow, coffee brewing, an orange sliced in four and a note that read, "Can I see you tonight? - Benji."

"Never date a married man," flashed in my mind like a neon sign. When you meet someone, before you even get to know everything about them, you already know if you like them or not, or if it was a total waste of time, by at least the second date. This definitely wasn't a waste of time; I tried to convince myself.

I loved this man, I found myself saying. Surely I was losing my mind. How could I go from being blissfully in love with Mark to surrendering my virginity to Benjamin? I tried to justify it all in my mind, but I couldn't. Love had no rules. I knew that going into the relationship. I know I just met him. I know it didn't make sense, but then it never does. I mean, it wasn't like he was in love with her. I guess maybe once he was. But it's what he feels now that matters. He said he cares about her. What I was doing wasn't right, I knew it. My conscience told me that.

He cares about her. I tried to imagine exactly what he meant by "I care for her." I couldn't. I realized that I could analyze the word "care" forever but it still wouldn't satisfy me. It was a complicated situation. There is no way I can or should logically give into this man again.

I wanted to believe him. I wanted to trust that everything that he was saying was true. When he looked at me and held me it was supernatural. I felt like Cinderella or the black equivalent. But, he wasn't mine. When was I going to actually find someone for me? Someone who was mine alone? Was he going to be mine or would I have to share him forever like I had unknowingly shared Mark? I had to know the outcome. I had to know it now. Mistress wasn't a title I desired or a label I wanted to wear for the rest of my life. I attempted to think it through in my mind. This type of situation took such a toll on your mind after awhile, and I didn't want to end up on a psychiatric ward suffering from a nervous breakdown just because I wanted a man I couldn't have.

It's not like I was attracted to him because he was married or wasn't available, I loved him because he's sensitive, he's gorgeous and he knows how to make me feel like a woman, in and out of bed. Sadly enough, most men can only do one or the other.

I prepared myself for work. Another day of making ends meet and cutting deadlines too close for comfort. Designs scattered across my desk, and presentations and phone calls to make, I couldn't wait to get out of the office. I had things to sort out in my mind. I had decisions to make.

Benji picked me up from work. He wore a mischievous grin. There was a chill in the air; the season was definitely changing. He escorted me to somewhere he said was a surprise. The thought of it all was theatrical.

"Keep your eyes closed," he said. We were in traffic, the radio wasn't on, but I was hearing music. It was getting closer and closer. Violins. An opera of some sort. Under the stars for an evening of enchantment, Benji was bringing out the woman in me. The opera was a surprise. I liked surprises. Benji and I chatted as the orchestra played. He brought wine, cheese, sandwiches and fruit in an adorable little picnic basket like the ones they sell at Pottery Barn or William-Sonoma. He fed me. I tasted kiwi for the first time and I loved it. We were bonding on another level.

I had always thought that kiwi was such a peculiar little fruit, or some man-made grafted thing. I mean, it was fuzzy like a coconut and inside had all those black little seeds, but it was exotic and delicious just like starfruit. I tasted starfruit for the first time last summer at Moma's. Moma would be pleased at how happy I was. Benji and I laughed and joked. It was wonderful, although I couldn't help but think about Rhonda and her failing marriage or what she would think of me dating a married man.

We talked about the other night. We made love and it felt so right, but "you can't ever trust the flesh" came back to my remembrance. He knew it was wrong but he wasn't happy at home. It hardly justified our actions. I thought of the myth of the greener grass and decided that I was just what he needed. I could make him happy, or die trying.

He was also struggling with the unrelentless efforts of not being able to get his book published. He had gotten so many rejection letters that it was giving him an idea for another book. "Rejection." A man's life of perpetual rejection. He also spoke of how he dreads going home at night. Messy home and a sink full of dishes, although that's hardly a reason for infidelity. He said that after they got married she started pulling away. Rachel. She's his wife, I'm not.

He said she never wanted to do anything or go anywhere anymore. His family would always ask where she was at all the family functions and he would just say that she wasn't feeling well. He got tired of covering for her and then they just started fighting about it all the time. He couldn't trust her and she could care less if he did or not.

He said that when they were dating he knew that she was seeing other guys, even though she always denied it. He admitted being in denial too. People always told him that he was too good for her. Several people said they'd seen her out with other men but when he'd confront her, she'd blow him off. She'd make lame excuses claiming that he was jealous and just didn't love her enough. He said he just wanted to be sure that he would be the only one if they got married. She assured him that he would be. He proposed.

He said that after he and Rachel had gotten married she seemed like she wanted to live the married life as if she was still single. Before the kids, she'd stay out late with a friend, which she never specified as being male or female. That was unfair. He had given his life to God two years after they were married and had vowed to keep every commandment, or at least try. She never made loving her easy, and she was dead set on making it as hard as possible for him to keep the seventh.

I felt sorry for him. Not pathetic, empathetic. He was a really sentimental kind of guy. Not weak, just caring. He deserved someone who wanted what he was offering. The whole package, not just the paying the bills part. We toasted to me getting put on the most coveted Brewington Project at work. William and I had designed a complex for a landowner in California who wanted a dual level structure.

We designed something resembling the Melrose Place units but with more of a Mexican villa feel to it. It had a pool too, blue and red tex-mex tiles were an option, but we weren't quite done yet. I had a lot more ideas for this project. William was my colleague, and nothing more. We worked closely together and sometimes a little too close at times for my comfort. He seems to have this thing for me. He keeps asking me out for coffee or lunch and I keep turning him down. Yet, it seems he still can't take a hint, more-or-less a direct "no."

We were, however, still the company tag team. We pulled it off. We faxed several floor plans to Mr. Brewington's office and they were ecstatic.

"Everyone will want to buy a unit," he said. He was really impressed with what we did with such a small piece of land. William and I had a hard time talking him out of a simple tenement building structure. He wanted quantity, we opted for quality. They loved it, they loved us, and needless to say, we got the account. Benji also toasted to us, and we smiled, though we were probably both secretly wondering deep inside ourselves if we were making the right decision by taking the next step.

He never brought up Mark. Never questioned me about him either, and I never asked about Rachel. His lingering kisses under the stars as the band played "Blue Danube" or something else vaguely familiar, put my mind at ease. I couldn't help but look into his eyes and tell him how much I loved him, over and over again.

"Thank you for another beautiful evening, Benji." I hugged him around his waist and leaned into him, feeling his broad shoulders tower over me.

"You're beautiful, Lea. Anyway I have fun with you."

"Really?"

"Sure I do. I'm even writing a book about it."

"No, you're not."

"Yes," he said.

"Really, I am. It's called 'A Warm December'."

"Like the Sidney Poitier movie with the girl that he falls in love with that dies at the end?"

When I got home there was a message on the machine from Rhonda. She wanted to come up for a visit. We all grew up in New York together. Village Cobbler on West 8th Street, summer basketball games, and the music they played in the schoolyard. She probably wasn't missing New York as much as she wanted to get away from her husband, Gene. Some people just weren't marriage material. Gene was a work-a-holic and just like in the movie *'Pretty Woman,'* he wanted to spend time with many different women without an emotional attachment.

"So why did the two of you get married, Rhonda?"

"I don't know," she said, "he asked me."

"That's not a reason, girl!"

"Look, Lee, I was twenty-two and I didn't know any better. He had a job, a car and wanted to get me out of New York, so I was game. It was either him or a broke brother with four gold teeth and no car," she laughed hysterically.

"Girl, please, there are men out there," I teased.

"How do you know? You haven't had a real date since New Year's Eve of 1989." She was funny, and I didn't mind being the butt of a joke every now and then. It was fascinating how Rhonda maintained a sense of humor.

"I'm coming up in two weeks, Lee, if that's okay."

"It's cool with me. What did Gene say?"

"What did he say when?" she mocked. "I didn't ask him, and I don't need his permission."

"Girl, you're crazy!"

"Yes, I'm about to become more than crazy, Lee."

And I knew just what Rhonda meant.

I don't remember the exact moment that Benji and I were deemed a couple. He appeared at my office every evening and whisked me off to a romantic getaway. I didn't know that there was so much to do in the city. We had ventured in and out of small art galleries and wandered the village to the tanners who custom made handbags and knapsacks. He wasn't ashamed to be seen with me. He made me feel important. We held hands, which was the simplest form of affection. Tonight was wonderful, though I couldn't help feel that no matter how perfect it felt, it was wrong.

Chapter Thirteen

I had to remind myself to give Pat a call. I hadn't talked to her in what seemed like ages. She had been falling in love with Sean all over again. They were living in a sort of honeymoon state. They were going out, just the two of them, and spending time talking. Love was in the air. I dialed the number that I had come to memorize, but when she answered the phone, she wasn't really in the mood to talk, I could tell.

"What's wrong, Pat?"

"This son of mine! I don't know what I'm going to do with him!"

"Why? Slow down Pat. What do you mean?"

"Well, while I thought he was still playing video games it seems that he's been having sex."

"Sex?"

"Now this little girl who he labels his girlfriend is pregnant! What am I going to do with a baby in this house? He has enough to worry about without worrying about girls!" Shame covered my face as I blamed myself for not sitting Pat down sooner and telling her about seeing the two of them hugging up in the elevator.

"He doesn't say anything, that's the problem. He says he loves her. I told him that love doesn't buy pampers."

"How is Sean taking it?"

"He's furious. He had plans for his son, plans that would tighten his future, not talcum powder and baby wipes!"

"Do you need to talk, Pat? I could come down and we could think things through, I mean, there are options."

"No, Lea, it's okay, really. I'm not in the mood to talk. I'm just too upset to even think rationally lately."

"Okay, well if you need me..."

"Yes, thanks, I'll give you a call if I need anything."

She was furious, I could see her frowning through the telephone. I had been so caught up in my illicit life that I had totally ignored everyone else who mattered. It wasn't right, nor was it an excuse. I could have prevented this pregnancy.

I had put my friends on the back burner since I met Benji. Every one of us had been long overdue for a girl's night. I thought that tomorrow night would be perfect. It took alot of coaxing for Pat, especially with what was going on with Justin. Sean convinced her that she needed time to kick back. So we did. We kicked back and watched movies, listened to music that I wasn't particularly fond of, and ate. Hotwings smothered with blue cheese, Josai made her famous curried shrimp, Nicky made rice and peas like Moma had showed her, and Pat brought her espresso machine and frothed us up a couple of cups. Nia bought lots of snacks, chips, dips, doodles and Oreos.

Nia's bruises were no longer evident. She seemed to be in high spirits. She was wearing a long black nylon spandex dress. She looked like she had a date, but then again she always did. We played cards, and after Nicky and I beat Pat and Nia at two games of spades, someone suggested it. Truth or dare. The girls squealed with delight, Nicky jumped up and started doing a little dance that she always does when she's excited. The butterfly. She wanted to go first.

"Ask me anything," she said, sprawling out on the sofa dramatically.

"The person to your right got to ask you the juicy dirt or dare you." Nicky was willing to tell anything, so I dared her instead.

"Aww this is gonna be good, girl," Josai said. She snatched up a bag of chips and adjusted herself in the chair. Joe was excited. I paused, not giving a hint of what I was about to say or dare someone to do. I glanced at everyone in the room and proceeded to dare Nicky.

"Nicky? I dare you, to call up Robert and tell him that you love him and you want him back."

"What?" She was losing her composure.

"C'mon, Lea, that's not fair!"

"Aww child," Nia clapped, Pat screamed hysterically and Josai laughed until she could barely catch her breath.

"And you must use the speaker phone."

Robert was her ex of almost two years. She didn't love him when she started dating him and she had never managed to acquire a love for him. He was handsome and employed, but she was into a rougher kind of man. She had the most difficult time getting rid of him. He sent her flowers, candy, lingerie and compact discs of her favorite artists. Despite her lack of feelings for him, she had slept with him on several occasions, which only tied the noose that she seemed to have around his heart, tighter and tighter.

"You make me sick!" she said, though I wasn't sure if she was laughing or about to cry. Nicky rolled her eyes and took the phone and methodically dialed the number she had dialed every day for almost two years. She pressed the speaker button and Josai and Nia giggled. Pat shushed them both. The pauses between rings seemed like years. On the fourth ring his machine picked up and Nicky sighed. She was off the hook. She smiled like she hadn't seen the sun in ages.

"You know you still love that man," Joe said.

"You should have left a message," Pat interjected.

Nicky giggled and thought it was funny that it was now her turn to truth or dare someone. She smiled at me but I knew that she had the scoop on my boring life already, she wanted the dish on someone else in the room. Pat smiled and Nia lowered her head, as Nicky looked her way.

"Josai! Truth or dare?"

"Truth," Josai said confidently.

"Okay," Nicky smiled, nodding up and down. Nia smiled too and listened contented and was a bit pleased that the question was not aimed at her.

"To whom and where did you lose your virginity, Josai?"

"Aww girl!" Nia said, coming to life. Everyone stared at Josai, munching and observing the uneasiness the question posed.

"Uh...it's been so long, I don't remember."

"Of course you remember. You never forget your first," Nicky sing-songed. Which was true for the most part since your first sexual encounter was somewhat of a milestone.

"C'mon, Josai! You have to play fair. Everyone has to answer the question truthfully," Nicky said.
Josai began to blush and lowered her closed eyes. She took a deep breath and then exhaled. There was a slight pause.

"Michelle," she said.

"Michelle?"

"Yes, she was a girl I knew in high school." Josai's face was red, but it was a liberation of sorts. She no longer

107

had to hide behind anything. Pat raised her eyebrows, and I smiled because I knew that what Josai was saying was not just for shock value, but was indeed true. She was a lesbian.

Nicky sat there in perpetual silence, lowering the bag of chips. She had no clue to the revelation her question would uncover. Nia nodded, she accepted everybody, no matter what color or sexual orientation. "Uh, when did you notice that you were different?" Pat asked, easing the question out there with careful consideration. We all wanted to know. Including me.

"I was ten and in the fifth grade and my best friend Samantha invited me to her birthday party..."

"Never mind. I don't want to hear this!"

Pat said, hurrying to the kitchen to refill the bowl of onion dip.

"God doesn't approve of that, you know," Pat yelled from behind the breakfast nook.

"Excuse me?" Josai said, visibly offended.

"God doesn't approve of what?"

"God doesn't approve of men sleeping with men and women sleeping with women. He doesn't approve of that whole homosexuality thing."

"Oh, I see. So as long as it's the same sex it's wrong, but if it's the opposite sex, then it's right?"

"Why are we bringing God into this?" Nicky asked.

"God doesn't hate gay people. God doesn't hate anybody, He hates sin," I said, not sure if I was offending.

"Shut up, Nicky!" Pat snapped.

"What are you, the poster girl for Christianity, Pat?" Nicky added.

"Believe what you want," Pat said snidely, "homosexuality is wrong and so is murder, abortion and adultery."

I sat up attentively, paying close attention to where the conversation was headed. I wasn't a murderer, a homosexual or someone who had an abortion, but an adulterer I was.

"We're not talking about abortion, murder or adultery," Nia interjected.

"I've dated married men," she added. "It's no big deal."

"Well I've dated men but none were married," Josai confessed.

"How could you date someone's husband?" Pat scowled.

Nicky said she had never dated a married man but that she's been attracted to a few.

"Lea? Have you?" Pat asked, pulling back the curtains to my secret closet and wanting to come inside.

A loud and persistent pounding at the door directed everyone's attention away from me.

"Nia! I know you're in there! Open up! C'mon baby, open the door!" It was Freddie and he was drunk.

"Girl, you better not even think about it," I told her.

She sat on the edge of the sofa, ready to leap to his defense. She said it was getting late and she thought that she should get going anyway.

"Nia! Nia! Please open the door!" Freddie wailed. The pounding was relentless.

I snatched the door open and laid into him something awful. "If you don't leave, now...I will call the cops, have you arrested and thrown into jail!"

He reached over me, extending his hand to Nia who sort of cowered and magnetically came to his rescue.

"Nia? What are you doing?"

"I'm going home. I love him Lea," she whispered.

I hugged her and spoke deliberately into her ear. "If he so much as lays a hand on you again, you better call me."

"I will," she promised. "I will."

Pat was sure that Sean was waiting up for her, and Nicky was noticeably exhausted, so we called it a night. Nia held Freddie up, and he leaned against her helplessly as she made her way down the hall with him.

"It's okay, baby," she said, "I've got you."

"I love you, Nia," he said repetitiously, "I love you, Nia."

Nicky took a bag of chips and looked around for something to put it in.

"Goodnight, ladies," Pat said, as she slid out the front door without as much as waiting for a response. I knew she couldn't wait to tell Sean what drama had transpired tonight. Josai, however, was concerned about Nia. She stayed behind after the others left.

"She'll be okay," I insisted. "She's strong." At times I guess I was a little over optimistic, but for now, I hoped I was right.

Everything concerning Benji and I was literally as perfect as a picture. He was doing freelance work for some of the major magazines and he thought that would help him get his name out there and his book picked up by a major publisher. He's been very busy lately, trying to find an agent that could get him exactly what he wanted, since the one he had didn't seem to have a clue or a following.

Slowly the daily ventures out after work had gone from every day to maybe twice a week. When we started this love affair he called me daily. Now days would pass before I'd hear from him casually inquiring on how I'd been. I figured that after the calm comes the storm, which didn't please me in the least. He had volunteered that he loved me. So why was I here now, wondering what I had done to turn him off?

I had his cell phone number, but it didn't offer any benefits. He didn't answer it when he was with me because she always wanted to call and check up on him and fight about where he was and sometimes it got pretty nasty. I'm not sure when this began happening, but now it was the norm. I mean, the things he said to her I never ever thought I would hear come out of his mouth.

"I'm a grown man and I'll come home when I get ready," he would tell her. Once he told her that he was never coming home. She probably knew it was only words, although I hoped it wasn't.

He didn't answer his phone when he was with her, out of respect for us both he said. Sometimes I didn't want to respect her, or for him to either, but I had to be graceful and ladylike. I didn't want to give him the wrong impression. I had his pager number, the number to his cousin's house and the number to his voicemail box, but it still wasn't enough, because he was hardly at his cousin's house and I couldn't track him down if I needed him by voicemail or pager.

"Money's tight," he said, so he limited his use on the cell phone, which I never thought meant me. But I began to realize that it did. Slowly but surely it did. One week he had gone without making contact and I thought of wicked things I could do to hurt him like he was hurting me. Maybe I'd send a subscription to American Baby, Victoria's Secret or Essence to his house. The name Aaliyah Braithwait on the mailing label would surely clue her in on the fact that I wasn't temporary. It was sickening and depressing. If I paged him when he was home he had to wait until she went to the bathroom or something, to call me back. And if she walked in the room while we were having a conversation, the conversation turned generic. So here I was sitting all alone and wondering whether to call his silly cousin and leave a message or to call him on his phone. I called him on his phone. After all he wouldn't have given me the number if it was really a problem for me to be calling. Besides he said he loved me, which to me is a green light for any and everything.

I dialed the number carefully, taking a deep breath since I had never needed an excuse to call him on his cell phone. I didn't know what his excuse would be for not calling me, but I was ready. The phone was ringing. A woman answered.

"Hello?"

"Hi, can I speak with Benjamin, please?"

"Who's calling?"

"A friend."

"A friend?"

"Yes, a friend...who is this?"

"Rachel, I'm his wife."

"Well...when Benjamin gets in can you tell him that Aaliyah called?"

"Well, what is this in reference to, Aaliyah?"

"It's in reference to being personal, okay? So I'm sure he'll know what it's all about." I hung up. My heart was racing, I was trembling and I really didn't think I could do this anymore. I felt so stupid. I had to hide. Why didn't I just say, "Honey, you're the ex-wife." I should have said that.

I should have told her, "Well, he wasn't your husband last night." Another reason I should stop listening to pointless music, it fills your head with tired old clichés. He didn't understand how painful it was. I didn't want to face her or talk to her either for that matter, that was his job, not mine. I'm beginning to figure that I'd better hold out for Mr. Available if I want the fairytale. Mr. Right was taken. I mean I want breakfast in bed, I want a dog, a boat and a summer home where the kids can go swimming in the lake. I want our name on Christmas cards and homemade eggnog.

I want him to move out and get his own place, that's what it all boils down to. When you were poor there were so many things you had to suffer through, and I guess an unhappy marriage and being locked into someone else's life just because you had kids together was one of them. He was a pawn in her game. He wasn't well off. His agent was still shopping his book around.

"Fire her then," I said. He said it wasn't that easy. People didn't want to read about reconciliation, they wanted to read about scandals, but he refused to compromise his writing. He had drive and ambition. I had to give it to the brother, he had a goal. I just wished that a divorce was more near the top of his list of priorities. Rhonda ended up staying more than a few weeks. She thought that all my agitation was directed toward her, though I assured her it wasn't. It was about Benji, but I could never tell her that. Moma would call and check on her, and Gene called a few times leaving messages too. We talked about Cheyenne and we decided that we shouldn't mention this whole drug ordeal once Chey got out of rehab. Rhonda, Nicky and I even went out to see a movie, just like the old days. *"The Truth About Cats and Dogs."*

"The truth is, men are the dogs and women are cats," Rhonda said. Nicky laughed but I, in defense of men everywhere and Benji in particular, I said it wasn't so.

We bought tons of shoes and sandals up and down West 8th Street. There's no place like New York for shoes. Hanging out, I felt like I was sixteen again. I was remembering when Rhonda would teach Nicky and I how to be ladies and how to sit and respond to a guy who paid us no interest. It was like a sisters-only slumber party. The only thing that was missing was Cheyenne. I loved my sisters. I just wanted them to rise to their full potential, and I realized I needed to do the same.

We got our hands dirty eating barbecued ribs and cornbread. Rhonda had about three Blue Hawaiians, Nicky had a Strawberry Daiquiri and a Pina Colada and I passed on the alcohol altogether. I had much more important things on my mind. I didn't want to dog men; I wanted to love Benji. I thought I could handle this situation, but as days lapsed, and I didn't hear a word from him, it proved to me that I couldn't.

The whole situation really didn't bother me at first, even though I'd rather he be single. But then after the phone incident I had to stand back and evaluate the whole situation, and it kind of started feeling like everything was always spur of the moment. I didn't like feeling like I was being shoved into an appointment book or clamoring for space in his life.

If one of his kids had to go to the doctor or was in a play or if something happened to her car and she needed his, we couldn't see each other. Deep down I think she played mechanic on the car just so he would come home, and he did. She knew there was someone else. She had to, and after the phone call she knew I was the one.

Regardless of how much time we had spent together in the past, I started feeling used and on the side and I didn't like it one bit. The novelty of me had worn off, I guessed, and I had to indulge in other things. So, I bought a car. I could afford to. I had money in the bank and no one to spend it on but me. It was a hip and happening metallic gray Mercedes, top of the line. Rhonda helped me pick out the color. "Go on, girl, spend that money," she said. A GI 857 or something like that. It was equipped with everything that Benji and I needed including its own personal copy of Maxwell to play on the car CD player.

I wear Versace suits, big deal. I wasn't rich, but it's what most people who make some real money do. They go out and buy it, and try it, to see if they can hang. Then when they learn to invest and buy smart, the novelty of being able to spend money like that wears off, and it's cool, it passes.

I always used shopping and spending money to fill my void, so did Rhonda. She maxed out Gene's Platinum Visa Card. I honestly didn't know it could be done. We went to F.A.O. Schwartz and she bought some things for Todd's kids. She was on autopilot. She bought Gene a couple of Joseph Aboud ties, and that's when I knew it. She cared. She was still in love. She was going back to him.

Thought we all tried to deny it, that's how love was. It grabbed you by the scruff of your neck and kept you face to face with it. You couldn't escape, you couldn't run, and if you did, you'd open the door to find it there waiting for you. Love was inescapable.

The Mercedes solved our problems for a while. The transportation part anyway. When he finally decided to show up, I gave him a set of keys to the car so there wouldn't be any excuses. He would call me to come and pick him up on the weekends because now her car was in the shop and she had his. She needed it to "run errands and keep doctor's appointments," she said. But, some days he didn't call and I'd wonder how he could go from wining and dining and saying he loved me everyday to calling to see how I was doing every three or four days?

He said his agent was trying to negotiate a deal, he was working on another book, and writing freelance articles. We shared a weekend at his editor's summer home in the Cape and wandered the beachfront looking for shells and listening to see if we could really hear the ocean in them. We enjoyed each other as if I was the wife, and it was forever.

A few friends of his invited him on a camping trip one weekend. He told his wife he was going alone, but he took me. We cuddled up the whole ride and you couldn't tell me that this man wasn't loving me as much as I desired him. We ate hotdogs and beans and thoroughly enjoyed nature for the two nights we were out there in the woods living like the wilderness family. We shared a sleeping bag and he whispered emotion-stirring notions into my ear as the owls echoed their whoos in the trees and he reconvinced me that he was mine forever.

We took in museum exhibits and it seemed that we were back on track, but at times he was preoccupied and it all means nothing when all that's left are memories and he has to go home to her. What he shared with her was real and what we shared together was part time, and on the down-low or "let-me-see-if-I-can-fit-you-in." It was fake and for the most part imaginary. It was beginning to feel like Mark all over again. I loved him, and it hurt me to say it, but I think we needed to see other people.

I'd find myself sitting at my desk, worrying and unable to think. I prayed for Benji to get writer's block or something, so we could spend some quality time together like we used to. You can't put someone on a pedestal and then kick them off. That's how I felt, jilted. I was desperate. I buzzed William and asked him if he wanted to go out for lunch. He was taken aback but eager nonetheless. He was like a catastrophe waiting to happen. What was going on with me and Benji hurt, but I still felt what I felt for him. I can't deny my heart, and I wouldn't try to either. I'm in love. Not to mention that's it's been the most meaningful few months of my entire life. I've never felt so adored.

People who looked down their moral noses at dating a married man had no clue. I didn't go out looking for him, he came to me. Freely and lovingly. And she would never understand that I never meant to hurt her. I wasn't like that. I didn't plot to steal him away - it just happened. This whole situation just happened. What can you do once you've fallen? I'm suffering more than anyone. I'd cut off my arm if it would stop the pain. Who do they think actually goes around looking for pain? Surely not me.

I never stopped and thought for a moment what God would think of my cozy little home-wrecking situation. I had brought hurt, pain and now suspicion to his wife's life. Though it seemed like she didn't deserve him, by law she was his wife, not me. I had to take a moment to reflect. I was out of control. Where had this caring Christian man who had talked in depth about religion gone?

It didn't help that he wasn't the typical married man fooling around type either. He was different. We held hands, we walked on the beach and we talked...a lot. He wasn't rushing me off to a hotel room trying to get a quick piece just because his wife was hardly ever in the mood anymore. I was driving myself batty.

"There is nothing a married man can do for me," I used to tell myself. It's like eating a sinful dessert and I wasn't about to feel forbidden. I want to be desired. Thoroughly desired.

But now I see the reality of it, and it's complicated. I'm not too enthused about the whole situation. He used to talk about divorcing all the time but now it seems that he's getting comfortable. Once he finally told me he was married, the desire to divorce her seemed to wane. He doesn't want to ruin the mood, or he'll say, "Let's talk about that later on in the week," and we never do.

Maybe he really didn't know me but I'm not about to live my life with visions of him making love to her like he had done me dancing around in my head. Wondering if he touches her or smiles at her the same way or drive myself wacky thinking that all I'm doing is making their marriage stronger by satisfying his needs and then sending him home to her. Either he was mine or he wasn't and as far as I could see, we could spend every day and night together and make love "Til the Cops Come Knockin'" but he was still hers.

Vanessa William sings a song that says "love takes no less than everything" and that is exactly what this situation was taking from me, everything. As romantic as I think I am, waiting in the dark with candles flickering just isn't cute. I don't believe in love at first sight but I do believe in love. And I do believe that he loves me, but he has to take steps in my direction if he wants this thing to work. I put my heart on the line, but what is he sacrificing? I can't even tell my friends about him because I'm ashamed. Ashamed and embarrassed.

I don't want people to envision hungry children in dirty diapers clinging onto the leg of his crying wife in the doorway just because we go out to fancy restaurants and go away on weekend trips. I could barely get through work nowadays and my creativity was zapped. I hadn't had my hair done in three weeks. This just will not do. It just wasn't me.

It wasn't my problem when he lied and didn't tell her where he was going. I didn't ask for this, love had just appeared on my doorstep and kept knocking until I opened it.

"I love him," I say, frowning and angered by the fact that the day was almost gone and I hadn't heard a peep from him.

William and I went to a little sushi place near Canal Street. It was more than obvious that I wasn't myself.

"So, Lea, what's going on?"

"Huh? Oh...I...umm...I'm trying to keep myself busy, and you?"

"Oh, well I've been looking forward to having lunch with you, for one. Are you still single?"

This guy didn't pull any punches and didn't waste any time moving in for the kill.

"Actually, William, I'm not single...I'm seeing someone."

"Is it that flower delivery guy?"

"What flower guy?"

"The guy who dropped the flowers off at the office a few months back?"

"He's not a delivery man, he's a writer," I snapped.

"Is he single?"

"What do you mean is he single?"

"I'm just asking, Lea, is he single?"

"No, he's not, he's dating me."

"No, he's not...you mean he's married, Lea," he said sternly. "He's not married, William."

"Lea, I know the guy. Well...I mean...I know 'of' him. Rachel, Dion and Aaron. I've seen him and his family together. I have friends who know this guy. I've seen him before at functions with his wife. So, if this is the prince you're counting on, forget it."

"Look, William, I have to go."

"Don't you want to finish lunch?"

"Lunch is all that this was, William. You aren't my type, and if I wasn't dating Benjamin I doubt it very much that I'd be dating you! So, you can sit here and play the Kevin Bacon game all by yourself."

"Well, that's fine, but I don't think that you should be busting up a happy marriage."

"What's so happy about it, William?" I said and stormed off. Let him pay the check. After all I did grace him with my presence.

Now I've gone and done it though, I thought. I'm a very private person and the last thing I needed was for the whole office to be whispering around the water cooler about how I'm a homewrecker, or how I take food out the mouths of babies. It's not my fault. I didn't ask for this. I needed a vacation. I needed to get away. Since when did I have to beg for attention? I didn't need crap from William or Benji! I just wanted to be alone, I thought, stomping through the crowded streets. It was near impossible to find a remote corner down here.

"Terry?"

"Hi, Lea, are you okay?"

"No, I'm not feeling well. I ate something at lunch and I think I've got some kind of virus or something, so I'm heading home. Tell Mr. Emerson that I'm going to take a couple of days off and to call me if he needs anything. Okay?"

"A couple of days?"

"Yes, two."

"Sure thing, Lea. Feel better."

"Thanks, Terry," I say fumbling with this cell phone contraption as it smashes to the ground. Tears were sure to follow.

I get in moods every now and then where I feel like I want to be away from everyone and everything, and this is one of those times. I'm not suicidal, but I just let the machine pick up all my calls. It's my way of coping. Leave me alone, is what I was trying to say. Rhonda called. Her flight landed safely.

"He missed me Lee," is all she kept saying. I guess when you got too predictable with a man it became boring. I was predictable. Go to work, come home, the end. I prayed for reconciliation for my sister. She deserved it. She never hurt a soul a day in her life. James called me too. The painting that ended up being dubbed "Mark's Mess" sold for about $650. Someone had put "Hurricane Mark" on hold but hadn't dropped the check off yet. That's when it happened. I became an artist.

Being an architect was artistic, creative and interesting but my passion was painting. I remember painting in kindergarten and it was great. Blue and yellow were my favorite colors then. It's only when society warps the minds of children that they lose their creativity, I thought. I wasn't that type of "make something out of nuts and bolts" artist, I was the "everyone can see something different in my work" kind of artist. The way I was feeling right now, I could create a couple more masterpieces. I had neglected all my friends for this man. I let myself work around his availability and his desires, and if that wasn't enough, now William is telling me, or insinuating rather, that I was evil and devious. I wasn't, but I sure was lonely.

I don't even know if Benji was really worth it. He'd probably love me and leave me for someone with perkier breasts, I thought. They never really planned on marrying any of us, you know. They just enjoyed the moment and loved how long it took for us to figure the game out. That's what I thought about married men who cheated. I knew I could find someone else. Someone who was available, someone who I could call at home just to say goodnight or sleep over with and make him breakfast in the morning. But why didn't I?

Why didn't I crawl out of the ditch that I was labeling love and find someone who could give me nine out of ten of the things I wanted in a man? I had a list. A man had to respect me, he had to be honest and affectionate, he had to be tender, romantic, ambitious and humble. He also had to be attentive, appreciative and available. Nine out of ten wasn't bad but the 1 thing he lacked was the thing I needed him to be the most.

So, why didn't I leave him? I loved him, that's why. I know I sounded like one of those pathetic women on the talk shows but I wasn't. I was sane and this was love. But I couldn't hold it in any longer. I was about to burst at the seams. I really needed someone to talk to now. I needed an objective ear and a voice of reason. I'm really trying to be strong but I should call Josai, I thought, as the phone rang and the machine picked up. It was Moma.

"I know you're there Lea, pick up the phone."

"Moma?"

"What's wrong, Lea? Are you feeling okay, baby?"

"Yes, Moma, I'm fine, I'm just feeling a little queasy."

"You need something hot to drink, child, like tea with honey and lemon. I hope you're not coming down with that virus that's going around."

"I hope not either, Moma, because I can't afford to be sick." "Did you call Nicky?"

"Not yet."

"Well, call her, she could pick something up for you and drop it off by you."

"Tell her to bring you some chicken broth or noodle soup. Okay, Moma." I guess when a maternal instinct kick in it never leaves.

"Get some rest, baby, and feel better."

"Okay Moma. Is everything okay with you?"

"Yes, child, I'm fine."

"What about Cheyenne?"

"Yes, child, she'll be home in four weeks."

"I called you at work first Lea, and Terry said you had gotten sick."

"Don't worry, Moma, I'm a big girl, I'll be fine. I'll talk to you soon. Okay?"

"Yes, baby."

"Moma?"

"Yes, baby?"

"Never mind."

I called Nicky. Today was Thursday and she didn't have a class until four o'clock.

"What."

"Is that how you answer the phone, girl?"

"When I'm sleeping," she grunted.

"Where are you?" she mumbled. "At home, I'm feeling a little queasy. Nick, I need you to do me a favor."

"Favors, favors."

"I need you to go by James's house to pick up something for me."

"Who's James?"

"He's a friend and an artist."

"Really?"

"Yes, really."

"Is he single?"

"I don't know, girl, why don't you ask him."

"I will," she giggled.

"Okay, I'll go, but I can't drop off whatever it is I'm picking up until after my class."

"That's fine, Nick, thanks a lot," I said, giving her his address and phone number.

"Moma said hi, Nick."

"When did you talk to her?"

"Just a minute ago."

"Is everything okay?"

"She's fine and Chey is doing great."

"Good."

"Okay, I'll be by later, girl, do you need anything?"

"A couple of cans of soup."

"Okay, Lee."

"Nick?"

"Huh?"

"Thanks."

"No problem."

I called James and told him that my sister would be coming to pick up the check. I also called Josai at work.

"Are you okay?" she said. She knows that I never interrupt her work, I always leave a message on her voicemail.

123

"No, Joe. I'm not fine. I'm at my breaking point. Call the men with the white suits and have them put me in the rubber room."

"What's going on, girl." I parlayed the chain of events down to the part where I gave him my virginity and the keys to my car. I told her about how he calls me on and off and that things are much different than they were when we first got together.

"I haven't heard from him in days, Joe."

"Call him then."

"I'm not calling him. When have you ever known me to chase a man?"

She said that I had to occupy myself. She said that by worrying I was making myself sick. I read too much into everything, she said. I probably did. Josai was compassionate. She was an ear and I could tell her anything. She said that she'd see me when she got off.

"Okay, but no funny stuff," I joked. "You'll be okay," she said, "you've still got that sense of humor."

I entertained myself with Montel, Jenny, Leeza and some gossip show called E! Television was a trip in the 90's. I ate saltine crackers and sipped on ruby red grapefruit juice until I dozed off right in the middle of "secret shockers-you thought I was a woman but I'm really a man."

Chapter Fourteen

Joe arrived in traditional friendship fashion with soup, hot chocolate, tea bags, honey, lemon, a newspaper, and Nyquil, which she seemed to think was a cure for everything. She heated up the soup and went into this whole deal about how she thought Benjamin sounded sincere and how she got the impression that he genuinely loved me, but she said some people just couldn't deal with this type of situation because it was very stressful and it required a whole lot of patience. More patience than I seemed to have right now, I thought.

I tried to explain the depth of the love I felt for him but she said that I couldn't let my love for him put the brakes on the rest of my life. I was unproductive at work, I spent no time with my friends, and I haven't been out on the town since forever. Attempting to change the subject I told her about the painting selling for $650, and she thought that it was a good idea for me to start painting again. It was therapeutic.

"It'll help you relax, where are your paints?" she asked.

"In there," I said, pointing to the closet.

"But, I'm not in the mood to paint, Joe."

"Well, get in the mood." She rummaged through the closet and pulled out my easel, three blank canvases and what had to be three or four paint sets.

"Don't move, I'll get it," she said when the doorbell rang. I may have problems with Nicky sometimes but one thing about her, when she said that she would be somewhere at a specific time - believe me, she was there.

Joe opened the door, "Hello."

"Hi. I'm Benjamin."

"I'm Josai, nice to meet you" she smiled, "come in."

She took his scarf and he was taking his jacket off. Her raised eyebrows told me that she was impressed. Very impressed. He's fine, she mouthed. I smirked and nodded my head.

"Lea, I tried calling you but your machine kept coming on,

and I called you at work and they said you'd left."

"I'm screening my calls, Benjamin," I frowned.

"Are you okay?"

"What do you mean by okay? Do you mean am I feeling up to par okay or am I emotionally surviving okay?" He was silent and puzzled but he learned the drill quickly. When I wanted to be heard he knew it. Joe picked up her cue rather quickly too.

"It was really nice to meet you, Benjamin," she said.

"Lea, I'll call you later, girl."

"Okay," I smiled. "Buzz me if you need anything," she said. "I will, and thanks huh."

Benji sat in the leopard print chair that I had moved into the living room. He seemed a little more than uneasy. Fear gripped me for an instant for what I was about to say but I could no longer be silent, if I didn't speak up he would continue to walk all over me.

"I just want to know what's going on, Benji! I haven't heard from you in three days and then you just show up here like I saw you yesterday! I'm not going to sit around and wait for you to decide to love me! I've got to know now exactly what you are going to do, and I need to know now!" I said, shaking my head with too much of an attitude.

"Now you know I love you, Lea."

"I know you say you love me, Benji, but that's not telling me anything," I said, pursing my lips, determined to get more than two words out of him this evening.

"Look, Lea, I'm trying to get my manuscript sold. My financial situation is kind of tight, and I can't do anything without money."

"I see."

"Rachel wants the car, and I'm still financially tied to the condo with her. I want to do the right thing."

"And just what is the right thing, Benjamin? Is the right thing leaving me alone in this apartment not able to pick up the phone and call you? Or do you just think that the right thing means taking care of her? It's always about her isn't it?"

"I have children, Lea."

"Yes, I know you have children, Dion and Aaron. But didn't you know that you had children before you started telling me that you loved me, Benjamin? What am I supposed to do now? Am I supposed to take a backseat not only to her, but to your children? Am I supposed to never be able to want to see you without feeling guilty? I'm not trying to separate you from your kids. I would never do that, but I don't think I can do this anymore, Benji."

"You just keep stringing me along and you won't give me a definite answer about anything."

"C'mon give me a chance, baby, don't give up on me. I'm trying to make things happen."

"Well, make them happen then!"

"Baby you have to be fair."

"Fair? Who's being fair to me? Is your time being divided into four fair?"

"Okay, okay, I'm going to tell her, Lea."

"Tell her what?"

"Tell her that I want out. Tell her that I'm not in love anymore and that the arguing and bickering has to stop."

"I thought that your marriage was borderline divorce already? Isn't that what you told me when we met?"

"It's been over, Lea, we've been apart for a long time. We're like roommates, nothing else."

"Does she know that, or is this just something you hope she'll come to realize?" He just gave me a look that told me I was pushing it, but his look didn't intimidate me one bit.

"Well, did she give you my message?"

"Yes, I got the message along with a whole lot of attitude, but I got it, and I'm sorry you had to go through that. I left my phone in the house and..."

"Save it, Benji."

"Lea, don't you think that when you hurt, I hurt?"

"I don't know, I'm hurting now, Benji, are you?"

"Yes, baby."

"It hurts to see you sad. I want us to be together. I want you to be in my life."

"In your life like how Benji? Like I'll see you when I see you?"

"No, like my wife."

"I want to marry you, Lea."

"What about your faith, Benji? I haven't heard you once even try to justify that in all the time we've been together."

"God knows I did my best, Lea. I can't justify it, I was wrong. But she doesn't want me. She never wanted me. She's just tearing me down and pulling me apart."

"I can't love a woman who refuses to see eye to eye or who won't let me be the head. She wants to wear the pants. What kind of man would I be if I let her? I can't handle that, Lea."

"Well, why did you marry her?"

"I don't know, I loved her, I guess."

"And what about now?"

"You mean, do I love her?"

"Yes, do you?"

"I care about her, but I could never live my life being tormented by her criticism daily."

"I know I got myself into this mess and there has to be a way out."

"Benji, I understand everything that you're saying but I don't know how much longer I can take this. You tell me such beautiful things, but I wake up everyday to a situation that is still the same. There's just too much pressure and you don't call me for days and then you reappear and I'm supposed to do flips and be tickled pink because you're offering me a spare moment?" "I know, baby."

"When you're here it's fine but when you leave it's too much to handle, Benji."

"It will change, very soon, very soon."

"It won't be long, he said, holding me in his arms as my tears began to trickle down my cheeks and dissolved into stains on his shirt.

"How do you know that she will even give you a divorce?"

"She probably won't want to but she has no choice," he whispered in my ear.

"It's not even a good environment for the kids."

"What do you think it feels like for me?" He looked me in the eye.

"My kids mean everything to me Lea, do you hear me?"

"If I have to take them, I will."

"You know she won't give up the kids, Benji."

"Lea, it's time that someone else besides her starts getting their way."

"I feel dead with her, Lea. She doesn't love me. I feel like she's keeping me around like some kind of novelty. I'm a man, and I have needs. I mean, if I thought that she loved me, I wouldn't have found you because I wouldn't have been looking. So, maybe you ought to thank her."

He held me so tight I thought for sure that he would cry too, but he didn't.

"Promise me you'll wait for me, Lea."

"Benji, I don't know what will happen tomorrow, but all I can tell you that I have to do what's best for me. I'm alone, and you have somebody."

"I've never felt anything like this before, Lea. What did you do to me girl? I feel like I've know you every day since I was twelve or something. I feel like we were born to be together."

"Do you really?"

"Yes."

"It's been that way for me from the beginning too, Benji. But why did you have to be married? Life would be so much more simple if you weren't."

"Life isn't simple, girl, but I love you, Aaliyah, and no matter what happens always remember that."

"Well, prove it, Benji."

"I will baby, I will. Thing are about to change for us."

"I hope so, Benji."

Chapter Fifteen

I had scheduled an appointment to see the doctor. All week long I'd been headachy. I was sure my blood pressure was normal, but the doctor wanted to take my pressure to make sure and do bloodwork to check my cholesterol, and run the standard profile. I sat in the waiting room staring at pictures that decorated the wall. They weren't as artistic as mine, and definitely not as colorful. In the waiting room there was a woman who had the most ferocious cold I had ever seen. Her eyes were swollen shut and her nose was reddened and enlarged. She needed a shot of something.

The doctor called her in first, which was good because I didn't think she should be walking around looking like that. She was infecting the whole waiting room. She was sneezing and coughing. She was touching magazines and passing her germs all around the room. I was already sluggish. I didn't need what she had. The doctor said I wouldn't have to wait long, and I'd be glad when he called me in, because I couldn't feel worse.

I was daydreaming of taking a vacation. I was mentally relaxing on a beach and ordering a Mai Tai or something just as exotic. I hadn't taken a literal vacation in almost two years. I was long overdue one, but William and I had this really important account and I couldn't blow it. After all, women fight to be treated equal and I had to maintain that I was worth my weight, if not in gold then at least silver. I had never taken a vacation with a man before either. I didn't know if Benji would be able to get away without his ball and chain following him to the airport or something equally dramatic.

I sat in the waiting room flipping through the same People magazine that was sitting on my coffee table at home. Josai lived for the People's 50 Most Fabulous People issue. Benji was fabulous. He should be in People. I thought about how perfectly Benji and I could love each other if we were allowed to. He could make breakfast and I'd do the dishes, although I hate doing dishes, but anything for love. When you'd gone without real emotion in your life, you learned to make sacrifices.

I wondered why doctors gave you appointments to come in to see them but then you never got called anywhere near the time you were scheduled. I was on time. I liked to practice being prompt. It didn't matter. I still had to sit and wait. Wait, wait, wait. After seeing the doctor, I had to wait to see a phlebotomist, and then I had to wait for the nurse again. The nurse finally instructed me that I needed to call tomorrow after twelve and that the doctor would give me the results by phone. I still felt sick. I wanted nothing to do with anything in a can. I was glad that I had brought a sweater, too, because the weather was changing and it was breezy.

In a sidewalk café on Columbus Avenue I sat and watched people walk by. For the first time in months I noticed other people. Women especially. I sat and wondered what kind of woman I had to be to get and keep this man's attention. I wanted him to stay, but only at his own insistence. Did I have to dye my hair, be more flirtatious, more mysterious or just ignore him totally? When you ignored them, they came running. This was as mentally draining as Josai said it would be.

When I got home I planned on having a pity party. Woe is me for falling for a married man and being naïve enough to believe that he would leave his wife for me. I should be put in the guillotine and have my head chopped off, I thought. Nicky arrived spur of the moment and was wearing her rose colored glasses of love. "Who is it this time Nicky?"

"You know him, Lee," she blushed.

"Your friend, James."

"James?"

"Yes! He's so sweet."

"Yes, and what did he promise you, Nicky? You know they always promise you something. How many times have I told you to believe it only when you see it, girl?"

"What's your problem, Aaliyah? You act like someone stole your best friend."

"I'm fine, I just refuse to get disillusioned by love and that whole La La Land concept."

"What about Mark?"

"What about him?"

"You really have a thing for him, don't you?"

"Girl, please, that thing is dead. It's been over for months."

"My Lord! I thought for sure that you would marry him. What happened?"

"What happened to what?"

"You and Mark."

"I don't want to talk about it, Nicky, can we change the subject?"

"Okay, well, how's Sasha, I haven't seen her around lately either?"

"Didn't I ask you to change the subject?"

"Yes, well I did!"

"Okay, Lee, I see you're in a mood and I can't stay long anyway. James is expecting me. We're going to a showing. He did tell me to tell you that your work is fabulous and that I should encourage you to keep painting."

"Well, I hardly ever get time to paint anymore, although I should. You two have fun though."

Alone. I was alone. It's what I had asked for. Silence. No annoying questions, and no mothering. I tried calling Benjamin's cell phone and it said he was outside the calling range. His pager must have been out of range also because he didn't return any of my pages. I hated pagers! Who was I trying to kid though? This man had had his fun and was moving on. I was a mere victim in his ploy to be entertained. And what an exciting summer it had been.

So I gift wrapped my heart and gave it to this man, he opened it up and pretended that it was exactly what he wanted and then he took it back to the store to exchange it behind my back for something more familiar, his wife. Loving was hard, you had to open up and put your heart on a freeway and hope it didn't get run over and scrapped to the side like roadkill.

Josai was the only one I could totally confide in. She was the only one who wasn't totally consumed with a significant other. Pat had Sean, Sasha had Mark, although I'd never call her in a million years, and eons after that. Nicky had James and Nia had Freddie. Josai was optimistic and believed that his wife had more to do with his minor exit from my life than I'd like to believe. I wanted to blame it all on him, but Josai was sure that he'd have some sort of rational explanation about why he hadn't called or come by lately.

"I told you that this type of relationship could take its toll on you, girl." I said I knew, and I thought I could handle it but I couldn't. I tried to read novels that I've been meaning to read, but found myself re-reading the first couple of lines of chapter one, over and over again. He was in my blood, under my skin, I was whipped, I was open and I was the village idiot.

Work was overbearing. William spent most mornings smirking at me in the office and I dreaded having to work with him. He smiled like he knew a dirty little secret. He acted like he had burst my bubble. He thought that he had revealed my little affair for what it was. Nothing more than an affair that would eventually end. They always did. He thought that out of loneliness I would come sniffing around him, which was a lie from the pit of hell! I wouldn't touch him with a used Q-Tip.

I tried to consume soup that Terry had ordered from a gourmet deli, but it wasn't going to happen. It was too hot, I had flu-like symptoms, and chills that forced me to walk around the office with a sweater all day long. "You should go home and get some rest," Terry suggested. But I didn't want to give William the satisfaction of claiming all the credit for the work that we had done together. They say that there's nothing like a woman scorned, well, I say, observe a man!

William walked around with his sole mission being to make me miserable. I hated his funky little attitude with a passion. He was obviously used to getting his way, but the only thing that anyone gets from me, is what I give them! He was acting like he was still in high school. I couldn't take it a minute longer.

I told Terry that I needed to leave early and that if Mr. Emerson needed anything to call me at home. "Sure thing, Lea." William walked by the office as I was heading out and backtracked stopping in front of Terry's desk. I could only imagine how he was trying to worm my whereabouts out of her. He needed a life!

Once I arrived at home I didn't take off my sweater because I had planned on heading out the door to pick up a prescription of something for this flu. I called the doctor's office and the nurse put me on hold. When the doctor came to the phone, he was cheerful. I thought of all the things that could be wrong with me that would explain my mood and the queasiness. The doctor said that I was fine and in good health, he also extended his congratulations.

"The queasiness is normal," he said. "It should pass after the first trimester."

I shook my head in total disbelief.

"There's nothing you can really take for it. It will pass. Try eating crackers or something tart, it will settle your stomach. You need to schedule an appointment with obstetrics Mrs. Barnwell."

"Miss," I corrected. "Miss Barnwell." And I couldn't help but think that at least Sasha had Mark.

Chapter Sixteen

Josai and I both thought it would be a good gesture to bury the hatchet with Sasha and Mark, so, before the year was officially, over I invited them over for Thanksgiving dinner. Sasha walked in the door looking like she was about to deliver on my carpet. And there was Mark looking as busted as the last time I saw him. Looking at him now I can't even comprehend what I saw in him. I was repulsed by his very presence. His shirt was wrinkled and he had started this habit of walking on the back of his pants. He looked like he needed to be marked down or put on sale so someone would take him home and clean him up.

So, now I had to forgive Mark. My feelings for him were merely fantasy. I wasn't in love with anything he actually did or was. I allowed him to use me because I thought that was all I was worth. I allowed him to play cat and mouse because I never thought that I would or could feel like this in a love that was reciprocated, although it was forbidden. The more I thought about it, the more I believed that Sasha and Mark deserved each other. She probably only wanted him because I did.

She was probably trying to show me that education and a good job weren't everything. But she wasn't going to rub my nose in anything, she could have him. Mark was, after all, quite boring. Not because he wasn't mine anymore, but because he really was. He and William were two of a kind. All he wanted to do was dine here and there, and he always thought he was taking me somewhere that I'd never been before. He would come over with movies, popcorn and that tired idle chit chat about friendship and how you never knew what could happen. Looking at them together didn't upset me tonight, it made me laugh. I had Benji. Even though he wasn't here yet, I had him. I invited Nicky and James too. It seems that they hit it off after she went by his place to pick up the check for the painting. Ever since then they've seemed to be an item. Inseparable. He called me and asked me if I would mind if they went out.

"Why should I?"

"Well, because you know we had a thing going on before," he said.

"James, that was hardly a thing. You two go on," I said.

They paired up at art showings, movies, dinner and most recently were planning a trip skiing in Vermont. The girl was getting a little culture. I guess now she can give up on watching *Red Shoe Diaries'* too. I invited Nia and Freddie to Thanksgiving dinner too, but she said she wasn't up to socializing. It was probably more his decision than hers. I can't help but notice how much that girl has changed. Far be it from her to miss a chance to hand out her business cards. So, I told her I'd put a plate aside for her. Pat, Sean and Justin came up, too.

Justin didn't seem too happy about having to be here, but Pat said she refused to let him out of her sight, which seemed to me a little like closing the barn door after the horse had already gotten out. He was a wild stallion but

138

he was determined to show his mother that he was mature enough to handle responsibility.

Joe and her female friend Nancy came over to help me prepare dinner. I didn't want to sound like one of those foolish women who says..."I love him and he's married but he's gonna get a divorce" so when they asked who I was inviting as my date I just said he was a friend I've been going out with. Joe smiled at me and I waited patiently for Benji to arrive.

I sat humbly gritting my teeth and trying desperately to construct a smile, while Sasha went on and on about how the sonogram showed that her baby was a girl and how she decorated the extra room at Mark's apartment with pink elephants and how she feels the baby kicking and turning around.

"I don't live in the projects anymore, I moved in with Mark. We're getting married," she announced, as if everyone in the room needed to know. She went on and on. Put a sock in it, I thought as I tried to grin and bear it.

"Can you pray over the food, Nicole?" I interrupted. James smiled like a proud papa.

"Lord, we thank you for our friends and family in our presence now. We thank you for bringing us together one more time. We thank you for this food, Lord, bless the preparer and those who do not have. We pray for those who are unable to be here today, Lord, and we thank you for the continuous blessings that enrich our lives. We thank you for Sasha's baby, Father, bless it and allow it to be healthy and strong. We pray for friendships that never change, Lord, and your grace that never ends. Amen."

I was not myself. The evening had dragged on and on, and a long evening that I thought would never end, finally did. I barely got through it. The gushing of new love was sickening. Not to mention that I was alone due to the fact that Benji didn't show.

"What happened to your date?" everyone kept asking me. If there was any turkey left I would have hurled it across the table at the next clown to ask that stupid question. Joe wanted to stay and talk, but I could tell that her friend didn't too much care for all the attention that she was giving me. She kept touching Joe like a cat, as if she was marking her territory. Thank God she didn't pee on her, I thought.

I wondered if Joe had told her about us.

"I'll be alright," I told her. Mark and Sasha left right after James and Nicky did. Mark helped her with her coat. A salmonish orange wool contraption that made her look like the great pumpkin from Charlie Brown, when she finally got it on.

"Thanks for coming, guys. I'm so glad you could make it," I overheard myself saying. I hoped that I wasn't laying it on too thick. Nicky took leftovers home, of course. That child can eat. She doesn't work out and she can still fit my clothes too. Baby, it's only because you're nineteen, I told her. Wait until you hit twenty-five.

Benji called me about 11:30 P.M., going on and on about how his whole family was there at the house for Thanksgiving dinner, and he couldn't get away. I'm thinking, what whole family? Benji wanted to know if I was upset and said he had no idea that she was going to invite his cousins and her mother over for dinner. It seemed like a last ditch effort to salvage her so-called marriage. He also said that he didn't think that the holiday was the right time to tell her anyway, and he thought that he should wait. The scenario unfolded. My life was starting to look like an episode of **90210** and I was about to cancel it.

"Is this the man I wanted to marry? Where had all the sensitivity gone?" Maybe this was my punishment for messing around with a married man in the first place. Torture, anguish and a sense of hopelessness. Me alone, gazing at my reflection on holidays and sleeping with the phone, waiting for it to ring, just so I could pretend that I wasn't asleep even if it was four o'clock in the morning and I really was. I could no longer let him be my world.

"Were people who married divorced people evil?" I wondered. It didn't seem like there would even be a tomorrow for us. There's been such a stigma attached to marrying a divorced person. Divorced people were treated like second class citizens. Other married people thought you probably just couldn't get it right the first time. It just wasn't true. The Bible says that God hates divorce. Malachi 2:13-16. I uncovered this bit of information after a little researching. I didn't know exactly what I wanted to find. Maybe I wanted to see if being in love changed or pursuade the fact that Benji was married and it was wrong to continue having a relationship with him.

I had spent hours in the bookstore alone the day after Thanksgiving. I browsed the relationship section for books on society's views of marriage and remarriage. $98.52 cents later, I had sacrificed my late nights to uncovering that God's ideal was and is a lifelong marital relationship marked by mutual commitment and love. People had their own views, which seemed to not always be in line with God's. I wanted to hear it from the source.

I was making a mockery of my life and my independence that I should have cherished. I was giving into a man that was someone else's without taking any thought to what the consequences would be.

"You'll go to hell," echoed in my head. It was close enough to what Pat had said when we were all together last. It started me to thinking.

I read a pink book with red roses, love was written in black cursive lettering across it. I read a book with people sitting on the beach as the sun set, and I also flipped through a book that had a couple's wedding picture that was torn down the middle. I was utterly confused. One Biblically based book went on to explain that divorce was permitted by the law "because your hearts were hard" and gave a scripture reference which I immediately jotted down. Matthew 19:8. In Matthew it was recorded that Jesus asserted that remarriage after divorce was adultery, except in the case of porneia, it said. Arrrgh.

I was puzzled at the fact that I might need a Greek translation to understand what I was reading. The dilemma was understanding what "porneia" meant. I wanted something simpler. I had a KJV, an NIV and a Living Bible. The NIV and the Living Bible were crisp and the pages smelled of freshly printed ink. I personally preferred the KJV although Moma had said that the NIV and Living Bible could be easier to understand.

I sat in the middle of my bed with the phone switched off; fresh air drifted into the room and a dozen books were strewn about the bed, all opened to their particular point of reference. It was 1:30 in the morning and I was consumed by the notion that what I was feeling for Benjamin had to be real. There had to be some way to comprehend what was going on inside of me. I had been known to be more sensible than to fall for someone or something that I could never attain.

The NIV translated the word "porneia" as marital unfaithfulness, which I made a note of. Matthew 19:9. It explained in the Bible dictionary that Jesus meant adultery, and that adultery constitutes grounds for divorce. But the dictionary defined a different Greek word "moicheia," as meaning adultery. The word is used in this same verse. This was extremely much. I felt silly to have to go to such lengths just to keep someone that didn't belong to me. The Bible dictionary went on to explain that it was best to take porneia as parallel to hardness of the heart, meaning here unfaithfulness to the marriage covenant itself. You'd be surprised what you uncover in desperation.

People would wonder what the alternative was. They don't want to divorce, but should people who hate each other and trade insults daily simply stay together for the kids? Will these kids grow up to be miserable and would the bickering parents in fact only be teaching their kids to endure suffering instead of how to love?

There were so many aspects of this thing called love that I had to analyze. It goes far beyond, "when he kisses me, I tingle." Love is a 'til death do you part thing. Or at least it should be when you find your soulmate, which I assumed that Benji and I were. How could he be my soulmate when he was married though? Beats me, but I believed that it would last forever. My heart spoke that. There was just something about him that totally got under my skin from day one and I haven't been able to shake it or him since. I mean, we've shared poetry readings in the city, the zoo, book signings, the opera, the theater, sunning on the great lawn in Central Park, every museum in Manhattan and a few in Brooklyn.

I've never felt this way with anyone else, not even Mark. Sure I guess from a moral standpoint I should have waited for him to leave his wife before we began our whirlwind love affair but hindsight is always 20/20. I didn't need to be reminded that what I was doing was a sin. I felt convicted. I had broken several commandments, not to mention the golden rule. He's the one who said that there are no kisses hello and no kisses goodbye. She doesn't greet him at the door and from what I can see she doesn't even want him until he wants someone else. So why do I feel like I'm on trial and my feelings are being scrutinized?

Why couldn't I like something or love someone without being analyzed about why I like it or why I felt it? White girl. They called me that. I had to explain to people why I preferred Degas and Monet to Leroy Campbell and Synthia Saint James. My entire life was spent explaining why I did this or why I did that. I had to explain why I preferred Toad the Wet Sprocket and Third Day to Gerald Levert and Karen White. I mean, I can tolerate anything when it comes to music, but I do have my preferences. That's exactly what I was doing, exercising my preference and my right to choose. I chose Benji.

But, now I refuse to explain why I love this man. I just do. That's it. I've thought about leaving him thousands of times, but it was only a thought. Leaving him would be about as much fun as standing in the rain and counting buses going by. Although that was just an analogy of how much I loved him. Our love was deeper than that. Losing him would be like losing a part of me or losing a friend I've had since kindergarten. I mean, it didn't make me psychotic enough to commit suicide but it sure made my thinking irrational.

My heart was in control here, or was it? From a scientific standpoint, the same feeling I get when I think about Benji is the same feeling one can get from stumbling upon a snake. My palms got sweaty, my heartrate increased and my mouth got dry. How could I tell the difference? People who were in relationships where the love had subsided no longer understood that love is a powerful thing. A very powerful thing. When you allowed yourself to overly enjoy the company of someone of the opposite sex, you were setting yourself up to fall out of love with your spouse. But that's not what Benji had done. He was out of love with her before he met me. I thought of all we had shared, and knew that if we never shared another second together, the memories would keep me.

Being alone made you listen for still small voices. Voices that left no doubt as to who was speaking to you. In the midst of all my irrationality I heard it clearly. "I shall be all you need." Tears comforted me for a change. I knelt and began to talk to God. I closed my eyes and rocked back and forth a bit. I wasn't praying, I didn't know what to say. I was wrong; I had to admit that first and foremost. Everything had to be done in "decency and order." Reluctantly I began flipping the thin pages and began to read something that was bookmarked.

I had this aching, instructing me that I needed to live as if I believed in something other than myself. I needed to survive for something more than just these feelings I had for Benji. I closed my bible, wiped the dust off of the black leather cover and pulled out loose papers that I had tucked in and folded in certain places. Lots of scriptures were highlighted and I began to review those passages first. If God couldn't help me, no one could. I read out loud and felt a slight calming. "Jesus wept."

Everything became clearer, not instantly, but clear enough to allow me to think about something other than Benji. I had to sacrifice what I desired most. He wasn't mine. It was like stealing. I couldn't unwrap a gift that God hadn't given me. I began to tremble as a heat flushed over me powerfully. I felt the presence come and touch my shoulder, telling me it was going to be okay, and I closed my eyes and felt comforted. There were tears that I believed were cleansing me. I wept unashamed.

The tears were dripping from my eyes and I couldn't control them. The more I tried to gain my composure the more they trickled down onto the pages. The inkmarks began to bleed. The tears of my past with Mark, my hurt and betrayal over what Sasha had done, my broken relationship with my sisters, and my dissatisfaction with the world that I had chosen over God for years at a time, were washing over me.

In that instance I felt like I could live, even if I didn't have Benji. I thought that he was everything I needed, but what I really needed was a deeper understanding. It wasn't about being deep, because so many people dwelled in religiosity and thought they were deep but didn't understand their purpose or calling. When trouble came to their brethren these deep people were the first to judge and throw stones. These deep people who should be rooted weren't and a gentle breeze could come and bowl them over, leaving them sidetracked and disillusioned. Everybody went through trials, who were we to judge the outcome of each other's lives? God was so much more tolerant than that, and for that I was truly grateful.

A frosty Saturday morning 9:33 A.M. A warm feeling hovers in the air like it always does when it's going to snow. All the school kids are outside trying to enjoy this last little bit of fall weather. The last of the colorful leaves are falling off the trees by the bunches and I'm wondering what he's doing. Benji. It's a constant fight not to think about him. I knew that I should be praying or meditating on the word but it was easier said than done. Benji was distracting. He had nullified my preoccupation with Mark. I wondered, is he lying in bed thinking about me here alone, or are they talking? Is he telling her about me and how he loves me so passionately, or is he just telling her it's over? How is he saying it? What is he saying? Is she throwing things like the good china? Or is he the most incredible liar, pretending with me and talking to her about how they're going to celebrate Christmas?

Alone in my bed I stare at the ceiling fan, trying to figure out how to differentiate what he means when he says that he cares about her but he loves me. Pacing the floor, flipping through catalogs and re-reading magazines from last year, my impatience begins to show. I've lost eight pounds in the last few weeks without even trying. I picked up the telephone to see if it was working and the dial tone just reassured me that yes, I was being foolish.

I went to the kitchen to make a sandwich that I knew I wasn't going to eat, because I was anxious and I didn't have an appetite. Smoked turkey with mustard. I was definitely going to tell him that it was over, I thought, wringing my hands and rehearsing out loud exactly what I would say. I was lovesick. He was making me lose my mind, though not totally. I didn't like it one bit. I didn't like who I was becoming. Where was the self-assured woman of power and grace that I used to be? If he decided to leave her, fine, if not, that was fine, too, I thought.

Shortly after 11:00 A.M. the phone rang. It was Benji, and I thought for sure I must have magical powers. The call itself at 11:00 A.M. was odd. He was hardly ever able to get out of the house that early in the afternoon because she was always there. I was more than excited to hear from him though, and the butterflies fluttered in my stomach as I hung on his every word. He said he needed to see me, which was refreshing. I wanted desperately to be someone's need. Lately I had been the one who wanted, required, needed, desired, and like a geisha girl, waited.

I felt like I'd never win this battle between Benji, my mind and God. I reached for my good book as if it was some sort of life preserver. I flipped through to a couple of pages and paused on Ephesians 5:25. Husbands are to love their wives "as Christ loved the church and gave himself up for her." I had to cross-reference everything if I wanted to fully understand what was being revealed to me. It said that the basic purpose of marriage is found in the bond it creates and the context for mutual growth it provides.

All he ever asked her to do is to keep the house clean and discipline the kids, but she couldn't manage to do either, and here I was feeling guilty. Why? Because I cared? I needed more time alone with God to seek answers and to finally feel like the loose ends were tied. He said he would be here by two. Sometimes I wish that he had never told me a thing about her. Then I would never be able to create an image of her in my mind.

I didn't want to recall things that he'd told me about her. I could care less where she shopped and how pretty she always looked for him when they were dating. I wanted to forget that they had ever met. I wanted to know that there was something special about me that had caught him and had drawn him in. I wanted him to be floored by my very presence, but as of late, he wasn't.

This was it. I was going to tell him that it was over. Definitely over. If he had to suffer with her for the rest of his life in a love that was leaching off of him, then so be it but I couldn't be his life preserver. He tied the noose around his neck when he married her. I mean, you couldn't save someone who didn't really want to be saved.

Moma called to let me know that Cheyenne had made it home safely from rehab. She was setting up interviews and I thought, what a waste it was that she worked at this insurance company for over three years, and now she couldn't use them as a reference. On the brighter side, at least she got her life together. Moma was right when she said that God watches over fools and babies. In my situation, I wondered which I was.

I stacked the magazines in the corner and boiled some cinnamon in a pot to freshen up the place. It smelled like cinnamon buns baking in the oven. I thought I could drive down to Brooklyn and get my hair and nails done at Black Roots before he got here. Evelyn said I wouldn't have to wait and that I'd be in and out in less than an hour. I was wondering to myself why I was getting a manicure if I was going to tell him it was over. Semantics.

The girls fawned over my car and made such a big deal out of a mere mode of transportation that I started to make a sarcastic remark about being materialistic. But before Benji that was me. I was just like them. Making a fuss over a label or a designer that lined his pockets with the money that I was foolish enough to spend on designs that seemed for the most part, mediocre.

On my way back uptown I peeked into the window at my favorite jewelry shop like I always do. I decided to go in and browse around at something shiny and gold. Meir wasn't in. I wanted to buy myself something extravagant like a diamond necklace and matching earrings for the elegant wedding that I thought that I would have one day. I had given my sister Nicky my diamond stud earrings and she thought that she was Princess Di now.

I was eyeing a pair of silver and gold cufflinks that I thought would be a perfect birthday gift for Benji. I thought they would make him look distinguished. Even though it didn't make sense to buy them when I was going to tell him that it was over tonight, I bought them anyway. When I got home I pulled out my gift wrapping box and wrapped the cufflinks in a fine purple and gold paper that I saved for my special gifts, like to Moma. I topped it off with a self-fluff gold bow and put on some music. When the bell rang, I knew it was him.

I tried to be calm. I took a deep breath, made sure every hair was in place, and opened the door.

"I can do this, I can do this," I convinced myself. His face was flushed and he looked as if he'd been put through the wringer. He hardly ever frowned.

"I told her about us," he said, before he even came in the door.

"Come in, come in."

"I told her everything."

He told her everything? He said he told her that he loved me and that he wouldn't allow her to begrudge him his happiness. He told her that somewhere deep down inside of himself, that teenage boy he once was loved her but he wanted out.

He said he tried to keep things calm, but people get so inspired by movies and television that the conversation got heated and he said she started throwing picture frames and flipped over the TV. He said that in anger she confessed that their second child Dion wasn't even his. The expression on his face disclosed that it literally broke his heart. I could hear the pain in his voice as he told me, and I could imagine how she taunted him.

As he continued telling me what she said, I could see tears well up in his eyes. He loved the kids anyway. Both of them, even if one of them wasn't biologically his.

"Go on! Go!" is what she had said to him. And when and if he finally left for good, it would be no one's fault but her own.

"Lea, can I tell you something?"

"Sure, anything."

"I'm so sorry. I know this is not the way that I should have conducted myself. I should have never put you in the middle of all of this and I should have never come on to you. I should have taken it to God in prayer."

"During this whole situation I should have sought Him. I thought I could handle this without him."

"You know we can't do that, Benji." He smiled at me, understanding exactly what the "we" meant.

I didn't want to disclose to him the results of my bloodwork. I didn't want my life to consist of trying to keep a man happy who wouldn't have bothered to pursue a relationship with me otherwise. I didn't even inform Josai of my dilemma. She would lecture me or possibly think that I had planned the whole episode just because I loved Benji so much.

"I've had to make decisions, Benji, I needed help. He has been there for me in the past and in this situation, I knew I could never make it without His wisdom and guidance. I need to make changes in my life, Benji, permanent changes." He nodded, trusting in what I was saying and knowing it was not only the truth but what was best.

I didn't want to hurt him. It seemed as though I was forcing him to choose but I wasn't. I wouldn't force him to do anything. I did however, want to know where I belonged and how I fit into the equation of his life. I wanted to find my place. I don't want someone's reason for not leaving their wife to be "I'm not in love with her but I want to be able to see my kids." I know that the way we are together is real. It's not just sex, it's love. But, would I never be able to protest him going off with his children everytime his ex-wife made him feel that he wasn't spending enough time with them?

Would I shudder everytime the phone rang, thinking that they wanted to steal another weekend from me? It seemed at times that he cares more about the financial obligation that he would have to his wife and the two kids than he cared about making himself happy. Especially since she vowed to make his life a living hell.

"If you leave me, I'll take everything," she said. "You won't have a dime."

"You can have it all," he said. But I knew that he didn't mean it. He had worked hard for everything he had. Nothing in life had been handed to him.

I understood everything, including his struggle as an aspiring writer. She wasn't supportive of him. Wasn't your spouse supposed to be in your corner? She wanted him to get a "regular" job, she told him, making *good* money. After all, their neighbors were all doctors and lawyers. In a nutshell she wanted his dreams of being a writer to die. And so she tried desperately to kill them by taking constant stabs at his manhood and his ability to provide. I'm not trying to say that he should be selfish by any means, but you only get one life. So it makes sense to fit yourself somewhere in the equation.

What could I do? What consolation was I to him? I longed to look down at his hand and realize that I am the reason that the band of gold is on his finger. Just to know that the ring he wore symbolized that I was his and that he was mine. He was gentle, kind and romantic. I didn't ask to fall in love with him. It was never money either. For the first time in my life it wasn't money. It didn't matter if we ate pate on Ritz crackers on the livingroom floor and rested our glasses on a coffee table with three legs. It didn't matter if it was raining or snowing outside as long as we had each other.

What we have is the type of relationship that you want your mother and father to have. This is the kind of love you wish for your best friend and for your children. We laugh, he tells me stories, he shares and he cares. Dare I say it's perfect? He is so tender that the sound of him coming near makes me tremble. It was difficult after Mark, but I still didn't know how I could have trusted someone with something so precious as my heart.

What Benji and I had was an illicit love affair, and though I wanted to believe that he wasn't just having a brief encounter with a woman, I couldn't. He couldn't promise me tomorrow, and I was just as unsure of today. I am not insignificant and neither was he. I genuinely loved him. Sometimes you look for love over mountains, in the clouds, under every rock and in the face of every man you meet, but when you stop looking that's when love does it. It catches you by surprise. It kidnaps your heart and holds it hostage.

I never expected to give myself so freely to a married man. Benji was everything to me. He was my nurse, my masseuse, my chef, my sounding board and my adequate lover. He said he wanted to marry me, and of course I couldn't tell anyone because people would have thought that I needed to be hit over the head if I really believed that. But like I said to myself, start hitting me because what we have is real and what we have is so unique I couldn't explain it. If I hurt him, I hurt me. I didn't want anyone to die or disappear. If his family matters to him then it matters to me. I wasn't hateful like that. I just wanted him, completely.

Moma often asked and wanted to know when I was going to get married. But if Moma knew what was going on she would kill me, regardless of how old I was. I would always be a child in her eyes. I wondered if our love was like this only because it was new? I wondered if the love that Rachel and Benji had was like this once? I guess I never really thought the whole situation through. I fell in love too quickly. I scoffed at love at first sight until it made a believer out of me. It hurt not to be with him and I didn't know how much longer I could take this pain. My life wasn't a soap opera but it was drama nevertheless and I wanted it to end.

I had become restless on this emotional rollercoaster I was on. One day I'm leaving him, the next day I'm loving him, but when I look to God, he reassures me that all things take time. God is the most important thing to me. I can't see Him, but I feel Him, and like the wind I know He's there. I believed that God knew I wanted to please Him. My happiness couldn't come from man; it had to come from God. I had been taking time out for daily devotion and prayer and I wanted to believe that my Lord would see me through. I didn't worry about what people said. They'd tell me, girl, you better rely on what you can see, and truly enough I could see God. He was working in my life and the outcome would be destiny. First God would get me through a day, then another one. Soon, all I'd need is God, not a man.

Why did I give myself to him? Were my hormones running things? Did I think I would lose him? Did I think no one would ever love me? Or was it just revenge against Mark? It may have been all three, but I hurt. The wounds were fresh and they hurt something fierce. I had rediscovered something that I'd lost, with Benji. Benji was an adventure in itself, the first of its kind. I was hooked. His love had its roots in me and pulled me from the core. I had to fight with everything I had not to cave in a die.

Sometimes when you loved someone you had to let him go. People who thought they were wise said that. They obviously underestimated how excruciating the pain of leaving someone you loved was. You have to suffer the hurt and just be assured that you are doing the right thing, they'd say. If he was yours, he would return to you. I prayed with all the faith I had left in God that the old saying was accurate. I prayed that the more I focused on the cross, the easier it would become to let Benji go. If I prayed hard and cried myself to sleep at night, the combination of the two would soothe me. I cared about Benji, I couldn't be abrupt. I had to be merciful, to myself as well as him. However, in the end I would have to forsake the only man I've ever loved thoroughly.

I believed that I'd die without him. I honestly did. Not me physically, but my heart. Some women held on and were patient and still didn't get the man in the end. Was that my fate? I was full of questions but I had no answers - no one to reassure me or tell me it would be okay. Every night I kneeled to God, seeking answers to questions I didn't really want to know the answers to. I already knew. With me in his life it was so complicated. Now that his wife knew he was seeing someone else she seemed determined to make it as financially straining on him as she possibly could. It wouldn't work, would it? After all, it was the oldest trick in the book.

We both knew that she only said these things because she knew that he wouldn't let his kids be without. I love this man indeed but if he still wanted to take care of her, then he couldn't have me. He said he would look for a place where we could be together, but how could he afford that? He had to make sure that his kids had someplace to live, clean clothes and something to eat. Especially since his wife was morphing into Broom Hilda. I have to be reasonable and unselfish. This will be the most difficult thing that I've ever done in my entire life, but I know that he'll thank me in the end.

If he loved me he would know that I only wanted to end our suffering. Not just mine, but his too. If she wanted him, even though he didn't want to be there anymore, and she knew that he didn't love her, then I was going to let her have him. I would release his heart to her, but then it was his choice where his heart finally ended up. She had betrayed him long before he met me. She shut down the lines of communication in their marriage. It was a tragic situation. Someone once wrote that it is better to have loved and lost then to have never loved at all. I think it was Shakespeare. He was right, and so was Nikki Giovanni who said, we love because it's the only true adventure.

"Benji? I need to say this." He looked around the room, his eyes not fixed on anything in particular. He was nodding for me to proceed. "I just think that this situation is causing more damage than it's worth."

He paused. "So, what are you saying, Lea?"

"I'm just saying that it must be this difficult for a reason."

"The reason being?"

I searched my heart for words that I knew would defy it. It didn't matter what I said, it would be a lie.

"I just think the reason might be that you need to be there at home. Your kids need you. Rachel needs you."

"Lea, I can love my kids and not be there."

"Yes but it's not the ideal situation."

"Life isn't ideal, Lea. What am I supposed to do? My kids will grow up, move out and marry. I'll still be there tolerating a dreadful situation."

"I just don't think we should make hasty decisions Benji."

Chapter Seventeen

Work has been more than hectic lately. Terry pulled me aside and wanted to know if I needed to talk.

"I still haven't been feeling very well," I told her. She was sweet, virginal in fact, but she could never understand my plight. She would probably douse me with holy water. William was still making it hard to work with him. He found it necessary to play mind games. He was hurt and offended that I had turned down his advances on several occasions. Although it didn't bother me at all because, along with the art of seduction, I've mastered the art of ignoring people. God wasn't finished with me yet.

If William wanted to act like a baby, then he could work those accounts by himself. I asked my boss to be paired up with Douglas, another guy at the firm that worked hard, was dedicated and determined to make it to the top. I was sort of friendly with him too. I proposed the idea to him first, he loved it.

"I've always wanted to work with you, Aaliyah."

"Really?" It was flattering. He didn't nearly have as big of a chip on his shoulder as William did.

"What about the commissions?" Mr. Emerson asked.

"It doesn't matter," I convinced him.

At first he hesitated, "Our clients are used to you two as a team, Aaliyah."

"I don't believe that I can give it my all Mr. Emerson. There has been and continues to be a conflict of interest."

So, he agreed to pull me from the accounts. I'd sign whatever I had to sign just to be done with William. When Mr. Emerson told William that I would no longer be working with him, he seemed even angrier than before. He thought he had me between a rock and a hard place but I won, maybe not fair, but square.

I was not about to mope around my apartment all night and then come to work and be miserable all day too. We all had a limit. I didn't plan on doing this much longer anyway. I figured, with what I had saved, I could last about two years without work. I was officially an artist, and I would begin painting in my spare time. James had opened a door for me.

"They liked your stuff, lady," James had said. And that was all right by me.

I dreaded having dinner alone again tonight, staring at the walls that still had paint near the ceiling as evidence of a not so distant episode. I might order Chinese or KFC. I was craving something greasy. I had breakfast, but it refused to stay down. I had lunch and it tried the same thing. I wondered what the baby would survive on if I couldn't manage to keep a meal down.

I wasn't psyched to be alone. I decided to run a few errands before I ventured into my dismal void called life. I went to my safety deposit box to take out the ring that I had foolishly bought. The flesh had me walk into the jewelry store like someone had given me a prophetic word that Mark would be mine. I was glad that I hadn't offered the ring to Nicky. Sometimes I can get carried away with giving and being charitable, then really regret it later. I decided to wear the ring and if someone decided to ask, the answer would be, "Yes, I'm engaged." William noticed it the next day at work. He never said anything, though it probably made him furious inside. He appeared at times to be on the verge of spontaneous combustion. Having me was definitely something he needed to get over.

I met Benji after work to talk and he noticed the ring too. I didn't have to explain but I told him about William and how I didn't want people asking me questions about him or feeling sorry for me. He understood, there wasn't anything he could do right now, but he understood.

"Lea, you're not my mistress. You know you're going to be my wife." I smiled, it was all I could do, so I nodded my head and smiled. Benji wanted to sleep at my place tonight. It would be the first time he stayed the entire night, and it would be nice to wake up next to him tomorrow morning and hold him in my arms. He wasn't mine legally but for the moment we shared he was. Only for the moment. It would be the last time I would be able to allow it. Things needed to change, and since he wouldn't make the first move, I had to. I didn't know or understand how I would manage leaving him, but I had to, or else I would never get over him.

He asked me what I was doing this evening.

"I have no plans," I heard myself saying. There I was still being available and ready. He told me that he had someone special he wanted me to meet this evening, and though I had no idea who it was, I was excited. We hadn't been anyplace together for a couple of weeks. I had met a few of his college friends and his cousin who I loathed, but he seemed anxious about it, so I was too. Was it a spark of hope? Or could it be the last hurrah? Things had seemed like they were dying down for us. The passion was fizzling and fading. It was all winding down and coming to an end.

159

There was nothing I could fathom that would resurrect his passion for me. I had to be willing to sacrifice all, like Abraham did.

We approached a white colonial style house on a quiet street in Mount Vernon, with a neatly manicured lawn and purple tulips that had bloomed and then begun to wilt in the chill of the changing season. Benji was silent the entire way. We just listened to a radio talk show and occasionally caught a glimpse of each other's eyes and smiled. Words had never escaped us before. We were reduced to glances and lowered heads. It had all become impossible for me to comprehend.

We observed children running down the sidewalk playing "steal the bacon" and debating about whether or not tagging a shoelace counted. An older frail woman with neatly styled graying hair answered the door; Benji hesitated for a moment then kissed her cheek. Hi, Moma, he grinned. Benji introduced me as a friend, which I was, nothing more. She hugged me and invited us in, urging us to have a seat, and slowly made her way to the kitchen. Her house reminded me of visiting Moma. There was always something baking. Something always smelled good and made your stomach answer when they'd ask if you'd like something to eat. She came back managing a tray with steaming teacups, tea biscuits and cinnamon rolls. Benji jumped to her aid, carefully balanced the tray, and glanced at me from the corner of his eye and grinned.

She was a thin woman with a radiant smile. She had her hair knotted in a bun and wore a simple dress that made her look matronly. She had adorned her mantleplace with pictures of her children in different stages of growth, a few of which appeared to be Benji with an Afro, maybe in elementary and high school. There was a picture with two boys; one of which I assumed was Benji's cousin since they had practically grown up together. There was also a family picture of Benji, a woman and two kids. Rachel. They appeared happy.

Benji's mom had a playful laugh. She joked and kidded around as she volunteered a few stories about Benjamin and his childhood antics. She told of how he loved to dance and garden, but not at the same time.

"He thought that if he planted an acorn a squirrel would grow."

"Mom you're embarrassing me," he shook his head. She talked about how he had waited on her hand and foot, and how all she wanted was for him to be happy.

"Are you happy, baby?" she asked.

"Moma, I'm fine," Benji offered, but it didn't answer the question. Benji told his mom that he was surrounded by wonderful friends and he sort of gave her the secret eye that meant, "Please lay off."

Benji was getting jittery and assumed that it was getting late, and his mom needed her rest. She was enjoying his company like old times. She assured him that she would be fine and that she looked forward to visiting him and the kids soon, an implication that was later explained by the revelation that Rachel hardly ever let the kids visit their grandmother.

"She always gets lost in Mount Vernon, Moma, you know that."

"Well, why don't you all come over for dinner next Sunday, Benjamin?"

"Sorry, Mom, we can't. Rachel has plans and I have to meet with my agent," he said in a feeble attempt at an excuse.

His mom wasn't pushy, and I could tell that he hated himself for having to lie for his estranged wife time and time again.

"We'll visit soon," he consoled. Benji was visibly fighting the urge to touch me around my waist and guide me toward the door. She made her way to the door and hugged Benji tightly. She knew that her son loved her, but like moms always do, she sensed that he needed something. She looked at me and gave me a smirk.

"You be a good friend to my boy, you hear?"

"Yes I will. He's very special to me Mrs. Braithwait." I lowered my head, thinking how much I hated to lie. I couldn't be good to him. It was over. It had to be over.

We drove back to the city with unspoken questions, which neither of us had answers for. I wasn't a golddigger; he didn't even have any money. What he had that I wanted, money couldn't buy. I wanted to please him, I wanted to undress him, and I wanted to wrap myself in the essence of his being.

I showered and changed into a comfortable robe, while Benji started dinner. He was a natural in the kitchen. I've always wanted a man who wouldn't wait for me to come home to start dinner after working a ten-hour day. Chicken with mushroom sauce, rice pilaf and a simple salad with baby carrots, radishes and snow peas. He snapped the peas while I rewound the video in the VCR. We had white wine and a little music with dinner.

"I didn't know you could cook, Benji." I smiled.

"My mother taught me everything I know."

I felt important, important enough to meet his mother.

I had borrowed a copy of *Up Close* and *Personal* from Craig. He thought I wanted to watch it with him.

"Craig, I'm having company."

"Oh, okay, okay. Well, maybe, next time then."

Benji and I ate solemnly. A candle flickered on the table in an attempt to put a little pizzazz in an otherwise dull evening. Benji conjured a decent conversation by asking if I remembered how we met.

"How could I forget, you invited yourself to sit with me," I laughed. He smiled, and took a more serious approach to the conversation. He pulled me up from the table as if he wanted to dance. We barely made it to the opening credits of the movie, when Benji wanted me to model what I was wearing under my robe. He had restrained himself all afternoon and evening and now he wanted to show me how much he missed me. I tried to fight the heat that was rising.

"It's only underwear, Benji," I smiled. Flirting was my forte.

"Let me see," he said.

"See what?" I joked, as he unbelted my robe, reached in and grabbed me around my waist. He kissed my navel, and his locks brushing against my stomach felt satisfying.

"What did you do to me?" he asked.

"Do how?" I blushed.

"You made me so crazy about you, girl."

I was getting excited, and I needed him to touch me now. I leaned my head back and my eyes were closed, soaking up everything he was doing to my senses. His cell phone rang, jolting us out of the moment. He fumbled for it and turned it off, seeming to prophetically know who it was. It was 12:45 A.M.

He paused and began to tell me about his mother and how she hadn't thought that he should marry Rachel, but he had insisted. This conversation came out of left field.

"I told her, 'I love her mom'," he said, sitting me down on his lap. He ran his fingers through my hair, but the conversation had already killed the mood a bit.

His mother said that the girl was a little golddigger, and that she was only looking for someone to set her up in a big house on a hill. He said he never saw it. She played the perfect girlfriend and appeared to be the busy little housewife until he started taking his writing a little more seriously. He said that she was a very selfish woman and that it was probably hard for her to imagine that he could take serious interest in something other than her.

"You're probably wondering why I'm telling you all of this."

"No, not really."

"Well, I just want you to know everything about me," he said. We got a little more than comfortable on the sofa. We finished off the bottle of wine and then drifted off, talking to each other about high school and other times when having money didn't matter, lying spoon fashion and eventually falling asleep in each other's arms. It was a moment that I had envisioned over and over, but was too late coming.

Morning found him making eggs and pancakes.

"Uh, I don't eat eggs, Benji."

"You don't?"

"No. I mean, I use them for cakes and pies, I just don't eat them cooked by themselves." He kissed me quickly.

"Okay, what about pancakes?"

"Sure," I smiled, "with cheese."

"Coming right up. You're weird, girl."

"I know," I giggled.

He said that he was going to go home, lay down the law, whatever that meant, pick up a few things and he would be back. I knew that sparks would fly the minute he went home. I told him that I had to go out to run a couple of errands, so I showered and got dressed in something comfortable but warm.

After breakfast I dropped him off and he promised to be back this evening. I figured that he meant that he was going to put Rachel in her place and withdraw money from a joint account and be on his way. How could I tell him not to? How can I let him see that his kids needed him there

164

with them? What if I changed my mind after he left her? He'd end up with nothing. I couldn't take the fall for that. What I had done was enough. I was ready to sing my swan song.

I stopped at the supermart. I bought yogurt, orange juice, saltine crackers and a newspaper. The tabloid in the basket read "jungle boy, half-man, half-ape to wed Elvis." The cashier had obviously been shoveled out of bed this morning, and wasn't in the mood to think too much. She had given me back extra change and twisted up her lips under her hairnet and headfull of pins when I gave her back the extra dollar and forty-nine cents. I should have told her that she needed to get some rest at night and stop running the streets. But who was I? I wasn't her moma.

I hurried home, sifted through my mail and poured a glass of orange juice. I was definitely due a vacation and wondered if Douglas was able to carry the accounts for at least three weeks. I needed at least that to sort what was left of my life from the mayhem. I couldn't be productive if I was tangled up like this. I was nauseous almost daily and if I ate another cracker I thought I'd turn into a saltine.
Mr. Emerson hadn't been pleased about my impromptu decision to take a vacation. I had waited outside of his office. He wanted to meet with me to discuss it.

"What's going on with you, Aaliyah?" he asked, instructing me to take a seat. He listened intently with a look of genuine concern on his face.

"I have personal matters to tend to, and I'm truly sorry for any inconvenience that this may cause," I apologized. "I wouldn't do it unless it was absolutely necessary, Mr. Emerson. Douglas assured me he can handle it until I get back."

"Okay, Aaliyah, but only three weeks and not a day more."

"Thank you, Mr. Emerson." I believed he was forgetting the six-figure revenues I had brought into his company over the past five-and-a-half years.

I decided that the relaxation process had to begin. I had gone home and opened up my paint cans, propped up the easel in the middle of the dining room and proceeded to lose myself in art for awhile. I stared at the blank canvas and began sweep strokes across the virgin canvas, creating something bizarre. But that was me lately. It was headless and colorful. A Venice De Milo concept, although it had arms. I didn't paint to sell the work and make money. I painted because I loved it and when it was done I felt like I had been baptized in serenity.

Benji called twice and I let the machine pick up. His messages were brief and convincing. But I was enjoying painting again. I was enjoying something besides Benji. It was scary, but necessary. My heart quickened. I had to quit him. It wasn't an option, it was for survival. I dared not return his call for fear of ending up relinquishing what little sanity I had left.

No one could ever imagine how it hurt my heart to hear his voice and know that I would never hear it again. To hear his voice say my name and know that I will never see him or touch him again was torture. To hear him ask a simple request that will never be fulfilled. I couldn't call him. That's what he wanted but I figured that it was better this way. I would go away for a little while. I'd give him time to forget me.

Maybe he could still patch things up with his wife. Six years was a long time. There had to be love there still. Deep down inside maybe. Maybe he really wanted to salvage what was left of his marriage. Maybe they could go to a seminar or something. Maybe I was standing in the way. Maybe he didn't know how to tell me.

I had made provisions at work and Douglas would be handling things until I returned. He was capable and I couldn't help but rejoice at the victory I had won over William. William was selfish, lonely and pathetic. Though I'm sure at times the same could be said about me.

Benji said he was coming back tonight. He was coming back tonight to a woman who no longer was. I would not be waiting for him like a harem girl to fulfill his every pleasure and stand hugging the doorway as he left and went home to his wife. I would not be preparing the perfect meal that would add fuel to the fire of the old adage that said his stomach was the way to his heart. I would be gone. The only thing that would linger was my scent on the knob as I closed the door on my way out.

I had never done anything this sporadic in my life. I had to call somebody. I couldn't just leave without so much as a goodbye. Nia had stopped returning my calls and was enduring her own hell with Freddie, and Pat was lost in the world of teenage pregnancy. Or at least her son was. I didn't call Joe because she would say that I was running from my problems and I was. She would be right. She was always right. I called Moma.

"How are you feeling, baby?"

"I'm fine, Moma. How are you?"

"I'm fine. Just a little tired."

"Aren't you getting any sleep?"

"Todd and Lisa sent the two oldest kids over here to visit for awhile."

"For what?"

"They're having problems. Lisa stays out all night, you know."

"What about Todd?"

"He's minding the other one."

I had to bite my tongue to stop from judging and criticizing. I couldn't stop her from doing what she wanted to do for her son.

"How's Cheyenne, Moma?"

"She's okay. Still clean. Met someone special she said, she spends a lot of time with him."

"Really?"

"Yes, she seems happy."

"I'm glad, Moma. Did she find a job?"

"Not yet, but she has interviews."

"That's great, Moma. It seems like everything is working out for her."

"God blesses Lea, He really does."

"Moma, I called to let you know that I'm going on a vacation."

"A vacation? When? Where are you going?"

"I'm not sure, Moma, maybe Aruba."

"Well, when are you leaving?"

"Tomorrow."

"Who are you running from, child?"

"Nobody, Moma, you know I'll call you when I get where I'm going okay."

"Well, who are you going with, Aaliyah?"

"I'm going by myself."

"By yourself?"

"I'll call you soon, Moma. I have to order tickets."

"Well, girl be careful. There are crazies out there."

"I know, Moma."

"Tell me baby, is it Mark?"

"No, Moma, Mark and I have been history. I just need to get away for awhile, that's all. I'll call you soon, I promise."

"Call me as soon as you get to wherever you're going, Aaliyah."

"I will, Moma."

I called Nicky and left a message on her machine. I asked her to check on my place while I was gone, she had a key. She wasn't in. Lately she never was. She spends alot of time at James's place. They were going at it hot and heavy. As I continued painting I thought of all the places that I would like to go. Somewhere tropical and nearly deserted this time of year. I decided that Aruba did sound inviting. It would be my destination. Peace, trees, exotic fruit and tranquility.

I pulled out my smallest piece of luggage, which was a Jansport duffle carry-on bag. I put a few light pieces of clothing, three books and a robe in the bag. I contemplated whether or not I would take his gift with me and decided what the heck. Nicky might find it and think it was for her. Shuffling through the newspaper looking for the travel section, I compared prices, circled one, and reached for the phone.

"I would like to purchase a first class ticket... Aruba...Charge...Do you have any availabilites for tomorrow? No, not round trip...one way."

Chapter Eighteen

When the reddish-orange sky cast its reflection on the restless seas and foaming waves lick up on the shore, you can't help but be at peace. Nothing I've ever known has been more beautiful or as invitingly tranquil as the warm Arubian winds blowing through those peculiar little divi divi trees. As I closed my eyes and inhaled the salty freshness, I couldn't help but envision being kissed all about the neck, shoulders, down my back and other places that mattered.

The sun slowly fades into the moon and the sea becomes playfully aggressive. I know here is where I belong, one on one with nature. Making myself whole again. Thanking God for each new day and relishing it without allowing myself to be bothered by the fact that I'm alone, even if it was by choice. I've had time for self-reflection and self-indulgence, as I rediscovered the carefree dreams I had as a youth. Slowly I can recall the things I wanted in life before I was sidetracked by the boys as a teen.

For so long I didn't know what I wanted or who I was. People, they tend to suck the life from you, every fiber, every being, and every cell. For many years I have suffered with the pain of trying to fill a void and tormented by the agony of not even knowing what was missing.

"You can't love no one until you love yourself," echoed in my head. I really didn't think it mattered then or that it even applied to me but Moma said this often. It just never sunk in until now.

I stumbled through my twenties falling in love with everyone else's ideas, goals, cars, men, schools, complexions, clothes, hair, pets, apartments, decisions, children, smiles, native lands and attitudes. It seemed if someone else had it, I wanted it. I forgot about being me. So, here I am in Aruba, tattered and torn, but cleaning house nevertheless, and the first to go was that little voice that kept on saying go ahead and trust him.

"He may not be rich but he's fine," or "Girl, he's the one!" the voice would say, which always ended up being a lie.

Lord knows I had my fair share, and then some, of fine, unemployed, no car, broke bums. Moma said that I was a bum magnet, and I probably was. But all that stuff doesn't matter now because I'm in love, with me. I matter and I always did. I was just too busy trying to be everybody else to notice. Deep down inside I realize that my desire in life is to be an artist. I guess it always was. I want to sing in a church choir, I want to run and operate my own business, I want to do any and everything else that people told me that I couldn't do, but most of all I want to forget the past.

Fourteen days ago I was a broken empty shell of a woman, left to dwell in the insanity that others who claimed to love me had created. Sure I've learned from those trifling traumatic experiences, they brought me to this point in my life so of course I appreciate it for that. Truthfully speaking I can't lie or deny it, of course I still think about Benji every now and then. Okay, well maybe even a lot. It's been two weeks, and yes I am a little sad about the way it ended. Benji and I had been through it all. I gave him the keys to my car and my virginity. Some things are harder to forgive than others though.

I could never take him back, not now; I've learned so much about me I have to move on. It's in my own best interest. I can't linger around waiting for someone to decide to love me. Moma said, "Never say never" and "Don't burn your bridges" and other "old folk" sayings like that, but I know what I'm talking about now more than ever, and it pleases me very much that this time I actually mean it. This year will be one of great change for me. "Out with the old and in with the new," my horoscope said. I'm not really into astrology but things were definitely changing. It was evident.

I ordered room service and sat at the window playing with my food and staring into the rhythm of the ocean. I still had no appetite. I had been here for days and never even bothered unpacking. I had a glass of champagne. One glass. I needed to celebrate life, or something. I decided to go for a walk and take in some scenery. It made no sense coming all the way to Aruba, if I was only going to stay cooped up in the hotel room. I walked on the beach. It was deserted. Slowly and carefully I wet my feet, remembering that there was a time when I had never been very confident or proud of my body. I had always wanted to change something, anything, and everything, but now here I was relaxed on my second glass of champagne, the wind in my hair and warm sand between my toes.

I slipped the straps off my shoulders and my dress fell down around my feet. I was proud of my full breasts, my hereditary hips and my evenly-bronzed skin. No, I wasn't a picture in a magazine that had been touched up to "their" idea of perfection; I was a living, breathing woman. A strong black woman I thought, and I wasn't about to

172

apologize for that. It no longer mattered that some of my so-called "brothers" thought my hair wasn't long enough or my eyes weren't light enough. Those feelings of insecurity I can finally say good riddance to.

Stacked, brick house, thickness, and other adjectives that were used to describe my body were washed away with all the other negativity as I waded into the water, a self-assured new me. I took the ring off and tossed it into the ocean. The ring that I foolishly bought for a man that I was naïve enough to think was only mine. It was symbolic of letting go of fantasies. I wasn't angry or upset; I was actually learning to experience the fullness of life. Especially the little things that others took for granted, like a clear crisp moon on a peaceful Caribbean night so breathtaking it gave you a desire to be closer to God.

I closed my eyes and silently I recited the sinner's prayer again. This time I searched the depths of my heart for the deepest part of me that could commit to God. That is the part of me that I needed to pray with. Lord knows I was a sinner. My life surely couldn't get any worse. I conjured every thought of God I could remember from my childhood. The cross, the crown of thorns, the blood that covers us.

"Forgive me," I whispered. "Forgive me."

"You are so sexy", someone said in a startlingly familiar masculine voice, that sent chills through my body, my heart racing and hands trembling. It must have been too much champagne, or else my mind was surely playing tricks on me, I thought.

"I missed you, Lea", he said softly as I tried to find the courage and power to turn around. But I was paralyzed. Slowly I was released from whatever held me and timidly I smiled. Unsure and afraid to look up into his eyes, my lips began to tremble as they always did when Benji touched me or came near.

173

He held me close and whispered in my ear, "I need you, Lea" and I stood there, willing myself to disappear as lonely tears trickled down my cheeks. He wiped one away and kissed the other. I can't give in, I thought. I was losing control, he was my weakness. He had always been. He made me feel. He made me come alive.

"Lea," his voice beckoned as he turned my face toward him and put his lips on mine. His lips were full, sensuous, moist and enticing. His thick brown curly hair was dreaded into strong locks. How many nights have I run my fingers through them? Do I give in? Again?

"I can't handle this, Benji," I said pulling away and scrambling for my dress. I closed my eyes tightly, hoping that he would disappear, but he didn't. I tried to fight it but he grabbed me and held me close, making it harder and harder to resist. There I was looking helplessly into his eyes as he held me in his arms.

I couldn't help remembering how I had always liked the slight curl of his lips and his perfect teeth that nibbled my neck ever so gently. But what was I saying? What was I thinking? I couldn't let him in! Out with the old and in with the new, remember? But now it was different, I was scared and terrified. Panic surged through me. They say be true to your heart and your heart will be true to you, and that's exactly what I had done. But all the pain and anguish, tell me what had I done to deserve that?

"Lea, I need you baby," he said, with such warmth, feeling and assurance.

"Oh, God, give me strength," I cried, as tears welled up in my eyes. Uncontrollably I blurted out, "I'll drown in this sea before I ever allow myself to hurt again."

His kiss silenced me passionately. I felt sixteen, and at that instant I knew. He could see right through me. He saw that my heart was still beating for him and always would be. I was lost inside his kiss, my knees were weak and I could barely speak.

"What do you want from me?" I managed to stutter, in a childlike voice that he had never heard, ever.   I was in tears and sobbing hysterically. "Look, just leave me alone, Benji," was all I could manage..."you hurt me, you hurt me," I sobbed.

"I know, Lea. I know." "

"You can't just walk in and out of my life like this Benjamin." He hung his head down and said nothing. There were minutes of silence between us. His strong masculine hands reached into his pants pocket fishing for something. He pressed a cute little black velvet box between my hands. "I want you to have this, Lea."

"What is it?" I mumbled. My hands were trembling as I opened the box to reveal the most perfect pear shaped diamond ring that I had ever seen in my life.

Kneeling in the sand, he held my hand in his, saying, "Lea, I'm sorry..." Tears streamed down his face now too.

Was I a traitor to my womanhood? I gently brushed his hair away from his face, searching his eyes for the truth. I looked into his eyes, and I saw myself. "My divorce is final. I want you to marry me, Lea," he said. "I want to spend the rest of my life with you."

The past was still so vivid and the here and now seemed like a dream. Benji was every woman's fantasy, even mine, and suddenly I realized I had lost the battle. I didn't have the strength to fight. I was weak, and I could never deny my heart, never. So I surrendered, I crossed the line. Love had captured me. Trust him, the little voice said...trust him.

Chapter Nineteen

I came to Aruba to get myself together. To put my life into perspective and weed out doubt and other things that didn't belong. I traveled far enough to get away from friends, so-called friends, and Benji. So why was I crying hysterically and why on earth was Benji here kneeling in the sand asking me to marry him? He's telling me that he had been selfish, that he's sorry that I had to endure the pain of waiting for him.

He said that she had served him divorce papers and he had signed them. He said that the lawyer assured him that he could fax the paperwork to wherever he was. After all these years Rachel told the other man that he was Dion's father. Now, he wanted to be a part of the child's life and hers too. Benji said, that he thinks they were still seeing each other behind his back the whole time. He's probably right. Though it didn't really matter now. Benji said that he still considers Dion to be his child and that he would still support both children. I know that he loves his two kids very much but he just wanted a chance to start over. He wanted another chance to love and maybe get it right by putting God somewhere in the equation. How can you wake up each day not loving? Waking up next to someone that should be there to support you, but was just tearing you down and criticizing you constantly, was hell, not love. Was it normal? I'm sure it wasn't healthy.

I asked him how he found me all the way in Aruba and he said that after leaving about twelve messages on my machine, he went by the apartment several times and he eventually caught up with Nicky. He said she was there with some guy, who was probably James. She told Benji that when she got to the apartment the ad for Aruba was circled, so she pieced the clues together and assumed that's where I was.

"What would she be doing in Aruba?" he asked Nicky. She didn't have a clue. But she called the travel agency pretending to be me, confirming what hotel I was staying in. Little Miss Nancy Drew, I thought.

"She sent this for you," Benji said. He handed me something that felt like a birthday card. I opened it. It was a birth announcement on pale yellow paper that read, Mr. and Mrs. Mark Stratford would like you to share in the joy of the birth of their daughter Monica Aaliyah Stratford, who came into the world weighing a healthy 8 pounds and 15 ounces on December 15, 1997. I was touched. They both had to really care to name the child Aaliyah. It was a step in the right direction. I had forgiven, and now I was healing.

Tears started to fill my eyes and I knew that by now Benji must think that I'm this weepy kind of woman. But honestly I wasn't. I really wasn't.

"Lea, I have a confession to make." I gave him a look that must have been reminiscent of the night he told me that he was married, and he reassured me that it was something that I would want to hear. He said that the day we met in the bookstore, he saw me sitting there through the window and he just had to meet me.

"Really?" I said.

"Yes."

"I thought that you just happened to be in the neighborhood?"

"Well, I was, but when I saw you through the window, I just
happened to be in the bookstore too."

We laughed.

"I've got good news too, baby," he said.

"What is it?"

"I got a two book deal!"

"Really?"

"They're going to publish my first book and allow me a year to produce the second one. Our story is my next book."

"That's wonderful, Benji! I'm so proud of you! Is it finished?"

"Is what finished?"

"The book about us."

"It depends," he said. "On what?"

"On what your answer is to my question," he grinned.

"Benji, I don't know if you're ready to get married. I mean, you just got out of a relationship."

"Yes, I know."

"So, are you sure you want to do this now?"

"Yes, baby, I am, but answer me one question. Why did you leave me, Lea?"

"Benji..."

"Why, Lea? You just picked up and left. I thought we felt the same way about each other?"

"I do love you. You know I do, Benji. I just didn't want to hurt anybody."

"Oh, I see. So you hurt yourself?"

"Benji?"

"Yes?"

"We're being honest, right?"

"Yes, I hope so."

"Well, I...I...I'm pregnant."

"Pregnant?"

"Yes, and I didn't want it to influence your decision in any way, shape or form."

"You're pregnant?"

"I mean, I didn't want you to stay with me because I was pregnant. Are you upset?"

"I love kids, Lea, you know that. I want you to have my baby. I want you. I want you, I want you, I want you!" He hugged me and started rubbing my belly. I brushed his hand away. I wasn't ready to start thinking about looking round or gaining weight.

I had to be only a month or two along. The doctor had said congratulations. Benji was a happy man, so, I was happy too. In the end I couldn't help but think that God gave me what he wanted me to have. A single man. I know it doesn't always happen this way, in fact, it hardly ever does, but then God knows that I didn't purposely set out to take someone's husband from her. Their marriage was on its last leg before I even came along. Before the bookstore, before the poetry and before the opera in Central Park. And if what Benji is saying about Dion not being his son is true, then Rachel violated their marriage a long time ago. I love him. And I didn't take him from her, she asked him to leave.

I called Moma to tell her the good news. All of it. I told her that I was pregnant and she went on and on about how she didn't even know that I was seeing anyone. I told her that Benji asked me to marry him and she said that if I was happy that she'd be happy too. She told me that Lisa had left Todd. Lisa had left the kids behind too. It came as a shock to everyone, except me. I knew Lisa would get tired of waiting around for that ring. Popping those kids out every ten months and Todd not having a job was enough to make you crazy.

Cheyenne walked in while Moma was on the phone, and Moma yelled at her, "Your sister's getting married."

"Nicky?"

"No, Lea."

"Lea?"

"Hi, Chey."

"What's up, sis?"

"How're you doing?"

"I'm finally getting it together, girl. It's hard but, I'm taking it day by day."

"Yeah, you can do it, Chey, I know you can."

"Thanks for the vote of confidence, sis. Now, who's this guy and are you pregnant?"

"Yes, I'm pregnant, his name is Benjamin and he wanted to marry me before he even knew about the baby."

"I can't believe it!"

"Congratulations will do," I kidded.

"Well, congratulations, girl!"

"Thank you. How's Florida?"

"Fine, how is New York?"

"I'm in Aruba."

"Aruba?"

"Yeah, it's a long story, girl."

"So, when are we gonna start planning this thing, huh?"

"Well as soon as I get back we can start planning this shindig."

"Are you showing?"

"No I'm only about two months along."

"Does Nicky know?"

"No."

"Does Rhonda know?"

"I haven't spoken to her yet. I'll make an official announcement when I get back."

"Listen, I'm talking long distance. Let me talk to Moma before I go, Chey."

"Okay, Lea, girl, call me."

"I will."

I told moma about Sasha naming the baby after me and she said that she would make the baby something nice.

"Moma, you were right."

"About what, baby?"

"You said to wait and I'll find love."

"Well, it seems like you went a little ahead of God, but we all make mistakes, child, and as long as you're happy don't worry about anything anyone else has to say."

"Thanks, Moma. I'll see you soon now. I love you."

"Love you too, baby."

Chapter Twenty

The sun is rising now, and the horizon is orange and blue. Joy overwhelms me and I can't believe that all this is happening. I lived my life to expect the worse, and if better happened, then so be it. We all want happiness and lovers, probably because we see them as something unobtainable. And for the most part they are. Happiness is fed to us by movies, television and books. Problems, struggles and misfortunes are omitted. Leaving us with a warped sense of what love is and isn't.

Love isn't waking up with a desire to trade in the one you promised to cherish. Love wasn't telling someone that you claimed to love that you wished they made more money or that you wished they were more like someone else. Love wasn't as trivial as that. Love was holding someone in your arms and wanting them even if they weren't perfect. Love was releasing your heart for a chance at forever and never regretting an ounce of pain it cause.

My eyes were getting a little misty and I was thinking to myself that this must be a dream. I love this man and he's here with me, what are the odds of that happening? He asked me to marry him, he's never been in jail, he has a job and he's a heterosexual, too. He began to stir as I sat looking out at the ocean and allowing myself to be swept away by the Arubian breeze, tranquil and calm. I walked out onto the terrace and the sand was a blank canvas. A place where no one had walked. I would have to paint this place, or as an artist would say "my interpretation of this place." Benji rolled over and looked up at me and smiled with his pretty white teeth.

"Is that why I fell in love with you?" I said.

"Why?"

"Because you have such a beautiful smile?"

"I don't know, is it?"

"Maybe." I smiled back.

"I made a reservation at the chapel for noon tomorrow," he said, squirming under the sheets.

"I'm having my lawyer fax the legal papers over to the hotel this morning." I sighed and I looked down at the ring on my finger and twirled it around and around a bit. It took great effort to manage a smile. No, not because I'm sad but because I am very emotional and on the verge of I don't know what.

"Don't you like it?" he said.

"Like what?"

"The ring."

"Oh, I love it!" I beamed. I never gave myself permission to be happy, so I had never been. But now I know that he is the reason that I was born. I had my experiences and he's had his, and it brought us to this place right here, right now. It wasn't coincidental. I didn't believe in coincidences and neither did he. It was fate. Destiny. We were created for each other. He was Adam and I, Eve. But we will never eat of the forbidden fruit.

It gave me pleasure to know that we fit so neatly together. So perfectly, so contently. This is what I've been asking for. It's all I've ever wanted. A man who was willing to go the distance, to fight for me. To challenge fate and create a love that knew no boundaries. He pulled me closer to him, and he held me with a longing that only true passion could evoke. When we take our vows I will have an assurance and a confidence in knowing that God had joined us together.

We didn't choose each other and we weren't forced together by unforeseen circumstances. He wasn't marrying me because I was pregnant and he wanted to make an honest woman out of me. It was inevitable. People had problems in what they thought was love because they weren't for each other, but we were. We are. We shall be. Tomorrow. The tears began to flow now as I thought to myself that I've never been happier in all my life.

He ran his fingers through my hair and assured me. "This is forever, Lea."

"I know."

"Will you marry me? Tell me you'll marry me, Lea."

I paused, but couldn't hesitate a moment longer. I nodded. "Yes Benji, I will marry you." Tears streamed down my cheeks and dripped onto the pillow, as I thought to myself how gentle and caring this man was. How completely he loved me. How he loved my mind.

"What's wrong, Lea? Are you okay?" I took a deep breath and began to explain because I knew that I could no longer be selfish, but in fact I would have to share my feelings for the two of us to be one.

"You know how sometimes when a person is so happy and overwhelmed with emotion that the tears are spontaneous and uncontrollable?" I asked. He was making his way down to my belly. "I'm that way, too, Benji. Sometimes I cry."

"Don't cry, baby. Everything is gonna be fine, Lea."
He smiled and those curious brown eyes told the truth.
"You won't, you won't lose me," he said.

We ordered room service and had to fight the urge to
share ourselves with each other physically. We thought that
we should start out on the right foot. I showered alone.
Although I would rather it had been our first time together,
this wasn't the end, it was the beginning. The water
soothed and caressed me; I embraced myself a loving
moment. I thought, "Hey, I like this." I could do this forever.
I was drying my hair when Benji answered the door. It was
room service. I pulled my hair back and pinned it into a
bun. I was inexperienced about what to do next, but I knew
that truth and honesty must reign. I was shuffling through
my bag for the perfectly wrapped box with the purple and
gold paper. Women have an honest-to-God sixth sense.

He tipped room service and sat me down to serve me
breakfast on my honeymoon eve. He placed my napkin in
my lap and poured my orange juice, which had a tropical
paper umbrella leaning in it. As he sat reading the
newspaper, I placed his gift right next to his coffee. He had
ordered pancakes with cheese and melon for me, and eggs,
grits and sausage with a side order of melon and kiwi fruit
for himself. Reaching for his coffee he caught a glimpse of
the purple paper and smiled.

"What is this?"

"Today is the second, isn't it? Happy birthday, baby!"

I sat on his lap and kissed him long and slow,
making him feel like the man I appreciated. Running my
fingers through his dreads and the tiny baby-like curls at
the nape of his neck, I was lost in him.

I kissed him just like any woman who has a man she
loves would kiss him. He was excited.

"Whatever it is, I like it," he said.

"Open the box, Benji," I insisted. He tore the paper off, determined to reveal what was hidden.

"Hey! They're beautiful, baby!"

"You really like them?"

"Yes, but..."

"But what?"

"But I kinda like you more, Mrs. Braithwait."

"Aaliyah Barnwell Braithwait. You know, I kind of like the sound of that."

"I thought you would."

I told him all about Josai, Cheyenne, Moma, Nicky, Rhonda, Lisa, Todd and my neverending quest for love. He told me about his mother who had inspired him to write, and his father's unfaithfulness to his mother that had made it so hard for him to leave Rachel once he had married her.

"She never loved me," he said, "I have to face that now. She married me for the show of it all." He showed me pictures of the kids and we sat up and talking for what seemed all night.

We talked about relocating to Texas, Arizona or California, and I smiled to myself thinking, tomorrow was a new day. The chapel at noon. I thought of life as I once knew it and then what I now shared with Benji. All else paled by comparison. He dozed off and I watched him, content in nocturnal bliss. He looked as if he had everything in life that he wanted, leaving not only his scent on the pillows but his essence and his being. I seized the opportunity, the moment. I sketched Benjamin, semi-nude, as he slept with the crisp cotton sheets draped so purposefully across his thigh and lower part of his back. I sketched perfection. Every crevice and curve. The moment was priceless. I couldn't wait to return home to wherever we decided to live and paint my sketch on canvas. It would grace the space over our fireplace. We had to have a fireplace. A modest home, it didn't matter as long as it was full of love.

The truth was that I was never looking for someone freaky who wanted to swing from chandeliers and make gorilla noises or someone who didn't have a clue. I wanted a gentle man who knew the art of love making or was at least willing to learn. Someone who was sensitive and romantic enough to give me a bath and all that other romantic stuff we often read about in magazines and change the way I viewed men forever. That's exactly what Benjamin did. He changed my heart, my mind and my soul forever, and I'll always love him for that.

Chapter Twenty-One

It had to be about 2:00 A.M. and I was sitting with my engagement ring sparkling reflectively in my eyes. He was offering exactly what I desired deep down within myself. But there was an uncertainty. It was unexplainable. I felt a gentle nudging and tugging on the inside, telling me to wait. It was leading me to believe that I shouldn't go forward. It was telling me to wait without an explanation of what I was waiting for. Whenever I allowed myself to smile and find comfort and joy in imagining Benji and I together, there was a tugging. It had come out of nowhere, and without warning. It was pulling me in the opposite direction, away from Benji. I felt something that I recognized so fondly, nudging to get my attention. It spoke firmly to my spirit, "no, not yet."

"Not yet what?" Panic quickened my breath as I sought a deeper meaning and unrefutable confirmation.

"No marriage for me yet? No, don't get married?" or "No, not Benji?" I tried to shrug it off and ignore it all together, but it would not go away. I tried to envision what our children would look like, and I was glad that he had come to rescue me like a prince usually does. I felt special. I looked forward to enjoying strolling on the beach with Benji and seeing the sights, but I was honestly disturbed. I wasn't sure exactly what it was, but I was tired of feeling confused. I deserved a little peace.

I had spent my whole life being confused about one thing or the other. I wasn't sure if Mark cared, and it turned out that he didn't. Now, history was trying to repeat itself with Benji and I couldn't endure losing someone I cared so deeply about, again. I listened to myself talking out loud. I wasn't sure what was going on here.

I took the opportunity on the beach to find some quiet time alone with God. After all, the void of God in any marriage doomed it from the start. I needed to know about "not yet" and if it was really God or just my fears. The enemy used your fears against you. I wasn't about to let what Benji and I had struggled with for months get unraveled. I watched a man running on the beach and his shoe prints faded away leaving little evidence that he had been there moments before. How unpredictable this life was, I thought.

I sat and listened to the waves crash on the shoreline and snatch away patches of sand as they returned to the sea. It was soothing.

"Lord, I don't want to be the same. I want to be sure. I want to know you in your fullness and your glory. I need to know what to do next."

Tears traced my cheeks and allowed doubt to convince me again that I was the only woman on earth that would not find happiness. But it didn't matter. Maybe on those chilly nights when the other side of my bed echoed the sentiments that I would still spend another holiday season alone, carving turkey or waking on Christmas morning with only me there to open gifts, it mattered a little. But right now, it really didn't matter. Not at all.

I knew that I could cry because there was hope for me and my Lord wants what is best. I thought I had found what was best. I believed that I had found what was loving, kind and dependable. Benji. Still small voices permeate your body and leave you powerless and trembling.

"If you want to know me, you must know my word." I felt the voice cut through me and strip away all the pretense and excuses. I could not use anger, or a lifetime of never getting what I wanted, as an excuse not to follow Him. I felt like a child, humble, submissive and protected. I prayed.

Back in the hotel room, I tossed and turned and managed to sleep and eventually dreamt. I dreamt of salmon-colored roses, tiger lilies and baby's breath that made up my wedding bouquet, tropical flowers courtesy of the chapel. I wore a simple all white slip dress, though one strap constantly slipped off my shoulder. I was barefoot and so was Benji. He wore flax-colored linen slacks and a white silk shirt that blew in the Arubian wind. Forever, I thought. This is forever. I wouldn't cheat and I would never turn down Moonlight and Valentino for the Shark Bar in New York City on a Friday night.

There was an island native, standing in as a witness to the ceremony. The justice of the peace or the island preacher, whichever he was was, fumbling around for paperwork.

"So, where are you all from?" he said, looking at us over bifocals that teetered on the tip of his nose.

"New York," we said in unison. He smiled and nodded his head. I was patient, I waited. The justice of the peace wore blue and red plaid Bermuda shorts under a black preacher's type robe, he stared at us and began laughing uncontrollably. The witness sat fanning herself with a tourist fan from Aruba as if she couldn't wait for the ceremony to be over. She smiled at me, and though it wasn't genuine, it didn't matter. I loved Benji.

I often thought that love was like a conquering game where you wanted something just until you knew you had it, and then you made room for it on a shelf. Love and feelings I no longer tried to understand. Feelings don't make sense. They never do. That's why people fall madly in love instead of sensibly in love.

I dreamt that the justice of the peace wouldn't stop laughing long enough to marry us, the next thing I knew I was at a pay phone trying desperately to call Nia, but there was still no answer. It had to be at least 5:00 P.M. there and I remember looking at my watch. I called Pat. She was still agitated and embarrassed at what Justin had done.

"No, I haven't seen Nia," she snapped.

"Guess where I am, Pat?"

"I don't know."

"Guess."

"C'mon, Lea."

"Okay, okay. I'm in Aruba."

"What?"

"I'm in Aruba. I just got married!"

"Really?" Pat said, and she started laughing too.

"Stop it, Pat. Why are you laughing?"

"You can never get married," she giggled.

"Can you call Nicky for me and let her know?" I remembered saying.

"Okay, Okay. But when will you be back?"

"Never." I began giggling uncontrollably. But it was a dream.

Chapter Twenty-Two

I woke to find Benji sitting on the terrace in the morning sunshine, reading the paper and sipping his coffee.

"And what time did you get in last night?" Benji asked.

I smiled at him, flattered by the worry in his question.

"Benji we need to talk."

"About?"

"About the chapel at noon...I can't do this..."

Benji's eyes met mine and he let out a long exaggerated sigh. He seemed to prophetically know exactly where I was coming from. He didn't want to rush me into anything. He didn't want to rush into anything. He knew I needed to be sure, and I appreciated that.

"Benji, I spent a lot of time thinking last night and I just think we need to make sure that your marriage is irreconcilable."

"She divorced me, Lea. They're faxing the paperwork over to the chapel. It's final."

"But have you divorced her, Benji? In your heart and in your mind?"

192

"Lea, you know I want to be with you."

"I know that, but if you were to show her love would she still feel that way? Would you still want it to be final if she loved you still?"

"You want me to love her?"

"I want you to obey God." It seemed as if the roles had been reversed and I was the one who was now rooted in my faith and Benji was the one who was following his emotions blindly. He wasn't concerned with whether or not I loved him, because he was certain that I did. He was just concerned that I was right.

We landed at Kennedy at 1:47 A.M. The halls were still decked with holiday trimming. It was cold, damp and I thought of all the things that I had to do when I got back. Nia was the first thing on my agenda. I had to see if she was all right, and I wasn't going to take a half-baked response as an answer to what was going on between her and Freddie. I had been reading a boring romance novel and anticipating stepping off the plane married and in love, but as of yet, I wasn't. I was still waiting and hoping. I prayed that it would happen. I wasn't so much worried about looking foolish in the eyes of my family. I was more concerned with losing Benjamin forever. Nicky and James met us at the airport. She seemed more excited than I was about the news that I was engaged. Cheyenne never could keep a secret. The trip itself had lasted almost 3 weeks, but it felt like heaven. I had gotten noticeably darker, and had done a lot of soul searching. I reflected on my feelings, wants and needs. I was trying to separate and prioritize the things in my life. I thought that I might even let my perm grow out. It was a good thing to be able to love yourself.

Lying out in all that Arubian sun and taking in all those rays, inhaling the fresh air, eating the ripe exotic fruits and getting cozy with someone I cared about was a God-send. I enjoyed watching some of the tourists windsurfing and scuba diving. I thought I was playing it safer to not participate, but Benji thought it would be an extraordinary experience, and it was. I had actually enjoyed all of the underwater marine life. The whole time I thought that I must be closer to heaven than I realized. I had Benji, I had God, and I loved me. It really doesn't get much better than that.

"Congrats, Lea!"

"Thank you, James."

"So what should we call you, Lee?" Nicky asked.

"Aaliyah," I said, smiling and showing off my ring. I was grinning so hard that my mouth hurt.

"Ooh, child. It's official!" she squealed.

"We're just engaged, Nicky," I said trying with all I had to be serious, but we giggled like we used to do years ago when we were closer. James and Benji were trying to fit the bags into the trunk of the car.

"What do you have in here, girl?" Benji said.

"Just a few things, so don't start," I teased. Nicky and I continued giggling about the endless possibilities of blessings.

I was exhausted from the trip. I slumped down in the car seat and yawned.

"Wake up!" Nicky said.

"We're going out to dinner girl. We have to celebrate. So, you can just go home, take a nap, freshen up and throw on something dressy."

"Not tonight, Nicky, please," I said looking down at my casual red and blue warm up suit.

"C'mon, Lee. You never do what I want to do! Just this one time, please Lee? Pleeease?"

"Stop using that reverse psychology. Is that what they teach you in school, Nicole? Manipulation?"

"Please, Lee? Pleeease?"

"C'mon, Lea, she planned something really special tonight," James interjected.

"Lea, she sounds like she went all out, baby," Benji said.

"Okay, okay, I'll go."

"Good!"

Benji pulled and tugged on our bags until he finally freed them from the tiny trunk of the Tercel that James was driving. Nicky and James were all snuggled up, and he kissed her gently on her forehead. She was obviously more a part of James than she would allow me to believe. I felt pleased that I had watched over her when Moma left. Now it seemed that she would have someone who would love her and walk with her through life instead of walking on her.

I called Nicky over and leaned into her, whispering "You're next, Nick." She nodded and smiled as if not to let on to James what we were discussing.

"Do you really think so?" she asked. I'm sure of it. I held out my arms, offering a sisterly hug.

"I'm so happy for you, Lea."

"I'm happy for you, too, Nick," I said, holding her tight and really meaning it. She held me it seemed for security, not wanting to let go. I was the only family she had here now. We shouldn't allow anyone or anything to cause us to become estranged. She was my sister after all and I didn't just love her because I should, I just loved her because I did.

I put my key in the door, dumped the bags by the sofa and observed the phone blinking, obviously with messages and inquiries related to my whereabouts. They would just have to wait. I had more pressing matters that needed my attention. Benji volunteered to sleep on the sofa and I gladly relished the chance to be alone in my bedroom. I loved this man, that was never in question. I was sure that this would happen for us but I was not sure when. Not that I didn't miss his touch or wish he was here with me right now, but there would be time for that later on. I just needed to focus on exactly what direction my life was going and what next level I was about to reach.

I ran through the things that I had to do when I got back. I convinced myself that I hadn't forgotten about Nia, I just thought that it was late and that I would definitely call her first thing in the morning. First thing. In between prayer and a little reading of the word, I fell soundly asleep cradling my pillow, pretending that one day soon I would no longer need a pillow that didn't offer warmth or arms to hold me. One day I will be blessed and joined together with a man. A man who is obedient, humble and lacks the normal male pride. Benji.

It was about two in the afternoon as the light invaded my sleep, but I awoke with an urgency. I needed to go to church this morning. I prayed as I got ready. "Thank you, Lord. You are the author and finisher of our fate." You would have thought that I was late for work.

"What's the hurry, Lea?"

"I'm going to church, are you coming?"

"No, I'm gonna read a little, I'll be here when you get back." He didn't think that it would look right for him to be coupled up with me in church so soon after his divorce. As far as people were concerned, he was still married to Rachel. No one knew any different. It didn't matter that he had the papers in hand.

We had forgone the ceremony at the chapel, but the front desk had received the fax from Benji's lawyer. The desk clerk had handed Benji the white envelope with scribbled red letters that read "confidential." We both knew what it was.

I called Nicky and got her machine. She was probably at James's anyway. I just thought that having someone walk in the familiar halls where I initially dedicated my life to Jesus would be comforting, but then God always has a way of taking us out of our comfort zone. I left Nicky a message that I couldn't make dinner. She would probably be disappointed, but I had lots of other things on my mind. I wasn't about to miss my blessing either.

I arrived at the church alone and nervous as the choir finished singing "Lamb of God." I absolutely loved that song. Jennifer sang the devil out of it. The spirit always moved when she sang it too. A heat flushed over the congregation and the Lord had his way. I missed that feeling. The lyrics allowed the presence of God to cleanse all within earshot. It was miraculous. Everyone has struggles, but in the presence of God they seemed to disintegrate, dissipate, they dissolved and He allowed you to be spotless.

The offering was received and I was feeling rather generous. The burgundy velvet covered baskets were passed up and down the aisles. You had to give to receive. I didn't have to worry about what the church did with my money. Once I gave it it was no longer mine, it was God's and He could allow them to do what they pleased. I gave in faith. I was obedient.

The service was spiritually moving and the word came forth with power. I saw only a few familiar faces; most of the people must have been new members. I embraced a few people and assured them that I had been fine. "How's your mom?"

"She's doing good, she loves the sun in Florida."

"I know that's right! You take care of yourself, Aaliyah." I forgot the sister's name but couldn't help but think that sometimes it doesn't feel very sisterly being a member of a church. People had a way of being territorial.

"I was here first so you stand aside and don't try to take over."

It was sad because I knew that it wasn't the way God intended it to be.

The sister, who had asked about Moma, she conducted the children's choir. She was friendlier than most, and from what I heard God had blessed her for her sincerity and dedication. She had suffered through several surgeries and the death of her mother, but now has a loving husband, a modest home and healthy twins. It was faith in God that allowed her to smile in spite of.

The choir was beginning rehearsal and a few members lingered about. I hesitantly waited for the church to clear out before approaching the pastor. Everyone standing around appeared to be waiting to engage him in conversation. He was overjoyed to see me. He waved.

"How's things, little Lea," he said, coming over and hugging me with the strength of a father.

"I'm fine, pastor. Moma sends her love."

"All is well?"

"Moma's enjoying herself for sure."

"Good, good."

"Can I talk to you in private if you have a minute, pastor?"

He led me to the second floor where his office was. I remembered the hall so well. Nicky and I had often helped out in the office and answered phones when his assistants went out of town, on vacation or to conferences. When the tent was going up in July we gave out directions and the schedule of speakers to the callers that flooded the telephone lines. I sat in the large chair by the window that always made me feel like a child when I sat in it. My feet dangled, not touching the floor and I tried to phrase the question in my mind but didn't know if it was worth covering up, so I didn't.

"Pastor, I need to know what spiritual steps should be taken before marrying someone who is divorced," I asked. Even though I'm sure he's heard it all before, from homosexuality to incest, there was still a shyness in asking my pastor such a question. I had never been very comfortable talking about such things. He nodded his head and his chin rested purposely in his hand.

"I would personally recommend a combination of fasting, prayer and counseling for anyone contemplating divorce, Aaliyah. Both parties should be willing to want to salvage their marriage. Two are yoked together in marriage, one can't carry the burden of wanting to stay together."

"I see."

"They must make a decision to at least try and attempt to reconcile before divorcing. Divorce should never be a solution to a problem that took years to get to that point.

"What if one party had a child outside of the marriage? Or what if they both did?"

"Forgiveness is the key, dear child. If they can forgive each other, they can get through that or anything else."

"Okay, I understand."

"Are you married now, Lea?"

"No, a friend of mine. He's really going through a lot right now." Pastor smiled.

"Would you just so happen to be the one involved with him, Aaliyah?"

Panic struck me as he was always led in the direction of truth.

"Y-Y-Yes," I said, lowering my head.

He said that he would like to pray with me, and asked me to have this gentleman come in to see him on Wednesday.

"He's a Christian," I added.

"Doesn't matter what he is. I told your mother that I would watch over you and your sister. I want to see him on Wednesday."

Pastor met with Benji. I wasn't supposed to interfere with the process of what Benji had to do. I was supposed to pray, so pray I did. Benji had to try and sit with this woman who had made his life hell, and attempt to salvage what could be saved. He began moving the few things he had brought back to my place after the trip, back home with Rachel. T-shirts, sneakers, sweats, a daily planner and his laptop. I fought back the urge to grab hold of him and never let go. He assured me that it wouldn't be for long, but through everything I just prayed that His will be done and that no one would get hurt, namely me.

Rachel had sold her marriage short. She had won the prize and instead of cherishing it, she had become unaffectionate, abusive, unsupportive and callous.

"Far be it from her to dab on a little lipstick," he said. Did that justify Benji finding comfort in me? No. Did Benji have a right to expect these things from Rachel? Yes. It was easy for Rachel to make excuses but a marriage wasn't a fairy tale, it was work. Hard work.

I was sitting staring at the wall, wondering what would have to happen before I experienced bliss. I listened to a song that reminded me of Benji and I cried into the pillow so the neighbors wouldn't hear me acting infantile. I had the right to cry, I had earned it, but I couldn't change what had to be done. I had to give him up if that's what it took. I had to let go if that's what God expected of me.

I was feeling depressed and alone. I finally gave in and called Josai, preparing myself for the verbal lashing that I knew was sure to follow. I hadn't told Josai that I was leaving for Aruba. She would be sure to lecture me just like Moma always did when I left without telling someone where I was going. Joe wanted to know everything, so I told her about the ring, the proposal, the counseling, my pregnancy and my ultimate rededication to my faith. She was happy for me. Not so much about the pregnancy that she assumed I might have endure alone, but more so about my reconciliation to God. She was so much like Benji in that they both had only my best interest at heart.

I told her about Benji's appointment to see my pastor and she volunteered to come over and sit with me. I felt like I was going through withdrawal and needed a sponsor. I had never judged Josai and her lifestyle, and she'd never judged me and my decision to fall in love with a married man. We were good friends to each other. We were there when we were needed.

Benji had been praying and fasting I'm sure, so he didn't call me. We needed to be apart, we both needed God's guidance. It's been four days now. His second appointment with pastor was tomorrow. I was nervous and on edge and didn't have an appetite but had to eat something for the baby's sake. The phone rang once but it was the wrong number and I almost lost it for a second. I picked up the phone and dialed the number to Benji's cellular phone twice. My better judgment got the better of me. I wouldn't know what to say.

"Come back?" That was pathetic. I had to be obedient regardless of how hard it seemed. I had to stand in faith.

I didn't have the energy or the desire to pray. I was being honest and I was bored. I began cleaning my bedroom. I sorted through clothes that I no longer wanted and some that I never wore and still had the tags on. None of them fit now anyway. I bagged them up for Goodwill or the salvage church, whichever could come first. I stood looking around at my bedroom, the bedroom that Benji and I had shared ourselves in. The bed on which we had made love and allowed Maxwell to serenade us. Now I desperately needed to hear track 8, "Lonely's the Only Company." But I didn't, it would only depress me more than I was already. I didn't need to sink deeper than I already was. Nicky called, interrupting my flow. I was thinking and sorting things out in my mind. She started talking about dresses and flowers.

"Slow down, Nicky. I have a headache, Nick."

"You always have a headache" she kidded. It wasn't funny.

She was calling me for a favor. She wanted to see what was going on in Florida and she didn't have long distance service on her phone so we hooked up a three way so she could talk to Moma. Nicky talked to Chey for a while and Moma said that Rhonda wanted me to call her the minute I got back from my impromptu vacation. I had received several messages on my machine from various people, including Terry, Sasha and Pat, but declined to return any of them until I was ready. I was going through so much now that I couldn't take the criticism or the questioning.

I had been praying a lot and had started reading "God Isn't in a Hurry" by Warren Wiersbe. I was on Chapter 20, "Forgiven and Enjoying It." It was enlightening to discover that true forgiveness was forgiving yourself, your brother and God. Most people thought it was just the latter. They were so filled with pride that they never humbled themselves enough to offer a sincere apology, and if they did manage to fall on their knees it was only in a selfish attempt to fake their way through a means to an end and have their blessing go unhindered.

I vowed not to be like that. I wouldn't fake it. I had my eye on how far He had brought me in this relationship with Him and knew that I had a long way to go still. But through it all I felt protected. I knew someone was watching over me. The Bible said, "Delight thyself also in the Lord; and He shall give thee the desires of thine heart," Psalm 37:4. I had held onto that scripture tightly.

Chapter Twenty-Three

Work had been very helpful lately in that it kept me busy and away from the telephone. I had to basically drag myself out of the bed and downtown to the office each day, but once I got there, I was busy until at least five. I was hardly what I would call a fashionplate nowadays. It was becoming harder and harder for me to get around. I thought back fondly to the days when Benji would show up at the office and whisk me off to a restaurant where violins played in the foyer. I was saddened by the fact that I didn't know if I would ever meet someone who could make me feel like Benji had. Someone so sincere and thoughtful that he made it almost impossible not to love him. He didn't necessarily have to come in a pretty package. Pretty packages were often empty promises. Which I didn't need in my life right now.

It was strange how obvious it must have been that there was a change going on in me. I had mellowed on the sarcasm and didn't once give William a dirty look. The water cooler clique had paid me little or no attention as of lately. It didn't matter to me as much as it used to. I was creating a dwelling place for joy to inhabit. I was thoroughly dedicated to this faith of mine. No one and nothing would ever steal my joy, I thought, placing a black, slightly worn, Nelson Bible on my desk. I didn't care about people's opinions on how they thought I was too deep. I wanted roots, and I wanted not to be tossed about with every whimsical doctrine. Jesus was black, Jesus was white, and Jesus was a woman, what trivial nonsense!

I had dedicated my life to a God that would do exactly what He said He would do. When man failed me, He would be there. When family judged and didn't have time to hear you, God made time. He did. I knew that it would be a process giving every problem I had over to God. "Lay your burdens at my feet," His word said. And I was trying. With clasped hands, I was trying.

Terry was her usual delightful self. She cornered me in my office and invited me to lunch. "I won't take no for an answer, Aaliyah."

Even though I was trying to be positive, I was still distraught by the separation that Benji and I had to endure until we resolved our situation in prayer. There was a great chance that we might not end up together. Terry was concerned. Terry wanted to make sure I was alright and I couldn't lie, so I offered her just that I was going through a lot emotionally right now. Especially with the pregnancy, I thought.

"Aaliyah, God will see you through this trial," Terry said, matter-of-factly. What Terry said caught me off guard, and I looked at her perplexed and unsure if what she had said to me meant what I thought it meant.

"You're a Christian, Terry?"

"Well, I believe in Christ and I know that He died and gave his life as a ransom for many," she grinned. I had thought of her in merely superficial errand-running terms and it seems now that she could be an ear. She was a lily in the valley, someone who would understand exactly what I was suffering through being obedient.

"I rededicated my life several weeks ago, Terry. I had been in a downward spiral."

"That's great!" she beamed. I was floored by the fact that I hadn't recognized that Terry's gentleness and humility were signs of how God had commanded us to be. Giving, loving and sacrificial.

Terry didn't walk around with a giant Bible and hit people over the head with it, but she was a light in an office that desperately needed it. I needed it. She was subtle and her faith was strong as she told me of how she had fallen into my sin, but knew that God had forgiven her and would forgive me, too.

"Christians aren't perfect, Aaliyah."

"I know, but people expect you to be," I added.

I was unsure of what sin of mine she was referring to since I seemed to have had so many lately, but I assumed she was referring to the most obvious one. I was not about to wear man's labels when the God I serve has declared me label-free.

"Sexual sin is what I'm referring to Aaliyah. I've been there." I didn't know whether she had discerned that, or if William went around the office whispering my indiscretions. I could not picture Terry in such a compromising position, but it just goes to show that you never know.

"Yes, there is a temptation," I agreed.

"But, we have to focus on the cross. There is so much we can lose by being tempted by momentary pleasures," she said. "I will be here for you. Just call me if you need anything at all, Lea, okay?"

I agreed that I would, and I meant it.

Terry and I chatted about the dedication it took to give your life to the Kingdom of God and leave behind anything that wasn't pleasing to Him.

"This life isn't it. This world is temporary," she said. She said it took a dedicated man to keep his head up when the world used it as a target. There had never been a moment when I could talk to anyone this freely about God or church. I smiled as I remembered how the word said that God meets you at your need. I went home with a renewed mind and I wasn't as depressed anymore. I had a breakthrough. There was a fire residing in me and I was about to let God use me up.

Rhonda always sounded like she had been running when she answered the phone.

"Hey, girl, what's up?"

"Lea?"

"Yes, Lea. Who were you expecting?"

"Where have you been, girl?"

"On vacation. Didn't Moma tell you?"

"Yes, but that was almost four weeks ago."

"C'mon. It hasn't been that long. Stop exaggerating."

"So, what's going on with you? I heard you're getting married?"

"Yes, but, I'm simply engaged for now."

"Well, who is Benji, and why haven't I heard about him before?" I paused, thinking carefully before I spoke words that were untrue or misleading.

"People don't usually approve of the type of situation that I'm in, Rhonda, and it's not something that I want to broadcast."

"What's the situation, Lee?" she asked sarcastically as if she already knew.

"I'm pregnant and Benjamin is divorced. He was separated but still living with her when we met. But he had been contemplating a divorce for months. When I went on vacation, he flew out to tell me it was final."

"What? Lea! How could you do something like that?"

"Like what? He didn't want to be with her. What am I supposed to do?"

"This man is somebody else's husband, Aaliyah. You should know better than anybody that that is not right!"

"He 'was' somebody's husband, Rhonda. 'Was,' not 'is,' 'was'."

"I can't believe that you slept with this man knowing that he belonged to someone else. That's just as bad as the women who sleep with my husband behind my back."

"Look, Rhonda, you don't understand."

"You can't make me understand why you would logically sleep with this man, Lea! There are millions of single men out there that you could have gotten pregnant by."

"Rhonda, I'm not going to argue with you. I'm just returning your call, that's all. Besides, I am human and I only have to answer to God for my actions, not you!"

"God? When did God find His way back into your swinging single life?"

"Goodbye, Rhonda, I have to go."

"Don't hang up on me, Lea...Lea?"

"The nerve of her," I said, as piercing shrills coming from down the hall startled me. I could hear it through the closed door.

"He's killing her, he's killing her," the woman across the hall yelled, pounding on her next door neighbor's door. Others were peeping out of their door investigating the sounds of a woman being tortured. Half-dressed, I stepped into the hall and began gasping for breath as I realized that the sounds were coming from Nia's apartment.

There was a thud against the wall and the sound of glass shattering.

"Don't just stand there! Call the police," I yelled, as tears streamed down my face.

"Nia, I'm coming! Nia! Nia!" I pounded on the door and I could hear her groan as he pummeled her. It was an agonizing sound to escape.

"Let me in, Nia!" I screamed, throwing my weight against the door. It wouldn't give. The neighbors clad in slippers and housecoats stood astonished.

"Do something. Somebody do something!" The sounds that came from Nia's apartment were terrifying, and I couldn't' do a thing to help.

The elevator doors opened and Sean and Pat ran off the elevator. Pat was hysterical.

"Do something, do something!" she cried.

Sean began pounding on the door, and threw his body forcefully against it attempting to gain access. The police finally arrived and announced, "Police, open up." They lunged at the door and it finally gave way.

Nia was lying still on the carpet, making no sound. Her face was purple and swollen. She was unconscious and was wearing a bathrobe, her eyes were bruised shut and her lip was grossly enlarged and distorted.

"Oh, baby," I cried. "Nia, talk to me! Nia? Please girl, say something!"

The paramedics wheeled a gurney into the apartment. "I've got a pulse," one of them said, kneeling next to her. He put her limp body onto the gurney and wheeled her out quickly. The neighbors gawked and gasped as Freddie was led out in handcuffs. He was noticeably drunk and smelled awful. His clothes were dirty and had blood stains all over them.

"Where are you taking her?" Sean asked the paramedics.

"North General."

Josai had arrived while all of the commotion was dying down. Pat and I sobbed in each other's arms. Sean filled Josai in on the gory details and Josai comforted us both.

"She'll be okay, Lea," Josai comforted. She was furiously upset, though I'm not sure which emotion took precedence. I made my way back into the apartment and got dressed as quickly as I could. I knew that Nia needed me. She was my friend and I had to go down to the hospital to be with her and help her through this. I should have been there for her, I reminded myself, as I said a silent prayer for her to be safe. God would protect her, she was my friend and I loved her, even if she had decided to stay with a man who was obviously violent. She could survive.

Tubes and beeping sounds gave me the chills. I hated hospitals. We were the only ones there with her. The nurse was on the telephone trying to contact her mother. The doctors huddled in the corner discussing her case. The nurse had started an IV in her arm. Nia lied still and was unrecognizable. She was bloodied and bruised over most of her body. I tried to be brave.

"God please help her," I prayed.

She was unconscious, her face was swollen and there was white everywhere. She didn't belong here. She was bloodied and limp. I touched her face. It was cool. I would help her recover. I could take an extended leave whether Mr. Emerson liked it or not. This is a family emergency; I loved Nia like a sister.

"Please let her be okay. I'll be there for her I promise." I tried to imagine myself in Nia's place, and I thought that it could have just as easily been one of us. We all gave more than we should for love. We all wanted the fairy tale.

Chapter Twenty-Four

At Nia's funeral I wore a simple black maternity suit and a lilac blouse. News traveled fast about Nia. I had spoken to Terry and she agreed to go along with me for moral support. Josai and her friend, Sean and Pat, and Nicky and James were there. Some clients that I remembered from the firm, who had become customers of "Dream Homes by Nia," were there too. Some faces I didn't recognize. Jack, Will, Darren and William from the office were there, they remembered Nia. I had introduced Nia to them a year ago at the office Christmas party. She wasn't interested in any of them, not in the least, but they thought she was a goddess. That was the same year she had met Freddie.

Justin sat in the back of the church with his girlfriend, who was now just a month away from delivering. Sasha and Mark walked in with their bundle of joy and I nodded in recognition. I couldn't help but think that if I had called Nia the minute I got back, maybe this wouldn't have happened. It was difficult not to think I could have prevented it all. I tried to concentrate on how she had always been a wonderful friend, and I was reminded that everything happens for a reason, but the reason for this tragedy eluded me.

There were over dozens of floral arrangements. I had sent lilies. Nia loved lilies. They were overshadowed slightly by the variations of red, yellow and white roses and pink carnations. People kept arriving to pay their respects to this wonderful and ambitious woman. I had never met Nia's mom or dad but I assumed that they were the ones in the front row, sitting next to a young girl who looked exactly like Nia, only younger. She had to be no more than eleven.

I tried not to look at Nia in the casket from the left side of the church where I was sitting. Gladly enough my view was partly obstructed by those that were brave enough to look into her face long enough to say goodbye. They had probably put too much makeup on her and I didn't want to see the Nia I knew looking puffy and strange. She loved life. Most people sort of moped through life, envying things they didn't have or striving for things they couldn't afford. Nia wasn't like that. I held back my tears. The anguish I felt wouldn't overwhelm me; I wouldn't allow it to, not today. I had said goodbye in the hospital. I would never forget her.

I prayed that Nia was in a safe place where there would be no more tears and where beauty would surround her, and where love didn't come disguised as balled up fists and hurled insults, but I didn't know whether or not I was just being sentimental and foolish.

Terry whispered that it would be okay. I just painted a smile on my face to hide the hurt I felt. I had never lost a friend before. I turned and glanced in the back of the church just then to see Benji walking in. He was wearing a long navy trench coat and appeared calm, and sort of deliberate in his pace. He noticed me but said nothing. I hadn't had time lately to feel sorry about what was or wasn't happening between Benji and me. I just focused on the thoughts and needs of Nia in her last hours.

Freddie had ruptured her kidney, punctured one of her lungs and fractured four ribs. With repeated blows to her head she had suffered a concussion, and the doctors knew she wouldn't live. An aneurysm is what killed her, though she had probably lost her will to live long before he had started on his tirade again. It was sad and pathetic that the man she chose to love had actually done this to her.

Nia's mother got up and spoke of how loving and giving her daughter was, and I agreed. She had never failed to be there when you needed her, she would give without you having to ask.

"It was as if she prophetically knew of the needs of others," she said. "She was hard-working and cherished life."

Her little sister began to cry. "No, mommy, no, mommy! Nia! I love you, Nia! Please come back! Please come back! Please come back!"

Her father escorted her into the ladies' room and the sobs for our departed friend echoed and began to fill the church.

The procession started. I had mentally chosen not to go to the cemetery. Once I told Terry about my pregnancy she didn't think that it would be too good for the baby to be under the extreme stress of watching a lowering casket. Everyone was gathering under the clouds outside. The skies were gray and it looked like a thunderstorm would have us knee deep in water any second. I stood dazed, unable to believe this whole scenario, as Sasha came up behind me and hugged me and began sobbing softly on my shoulder. I held her. We were after all bigger than a single isolated incident. Mark smiled and baby Aaliyah cooed. I thanked her for the honor of naming her baby after me.

"Call me," I said.

"I will, Lea. I love you, girl," she said, smiling and rubbing my belly.

"You're Aaliyah, right?" a tall brown-complexioned stranger said.

"Yes, I am."

"I'm Lance. I'm a friend of Nia's."

"Oh, yes, I remember, you sent flowers."

"Yes. I had no idea this was going on, did you?"

"Well, she did have problems with Freddie."

"I thought she was just brushing me off," he said. "I truly misjudged her."

"She was a wonderful person, Lance, that much I can tell you. She would be lucky to have someone who sincerely cared about her."

"I did. I really cared about her."

"I'm sure you did, everyone loved her. We were like sisters."

I was fighting tears that would surely have me doubled over any second. He nodded.

"It's nice to meet you finally, Lance, keep in touch, will you?"

"I sure will, Aaliyah."

"Great, I think she'd want us to be friends," I said, scribbling my number on a wrinkled piece of paper.

The skies were overcast and the clouds opened up. It began to drizzle steadily and Benji stood off to the side of the church, giving clear passage to those who were exiting. He appeared to be waiting for me to finish talking with Lance, so, I walked over and smiled cautiously. I was unsure of what to say or do, so I stood motionless waiting for him to cue me.

He stood tall, looking into my eyes.

"How are you, Lea?"

"I'm fine Benji. How are you?"

213

"Miserable."

"Really?"

"Yes, I tried Lea. I really tried..." he said shaking his head.

"But I can't make Rachel want to stay with me. I know I was supposed to stay there and try to see if I could work things out with her but..." I motioned for Terry and waved her on that she could go to the cemetery without me.

"Are you sure?" she mouthed. I nodded, yes.

"I have been at my mom's house for the past four weeks," he said. "The divorce has been final for months now Lea. Rachel moved Dion's biological father into the apartment and refused to meet me for counseling. I can't force her to take me back. She piled all of my things in the hall and demanded that I pick up everything immediately. The woman has totally lost her mind. I only wish I had seen this coming, before I married her. She's not what I thought she was at all."

"I'm sorry to hear about what's going on, I'll always be here if you need me," I said calmly. Trying to deny that inside I was tickled pink to hear that he wasn't living with her for the past few weeks. In my mind all I could envision was a joyous reunion and loving words being spoken between them, but then it was not my will. I had to comply.

"I know you probably wonder why I haven't called you and want to know what I've been doing."

"Not really," I lied.

"Uh, well, yes," I confessed.

"Why didn't you at least call me Benji?"

"Lea, I love you. I've been praying and it hurt not being able to see you or feel my baby. Your pastor thought it would be best to give you and me both time to reflect on whether or not we wanted to get into a relationship so soon. I needed time to heal."

214

"Some things have changed, Lea, and some things haven't."

"Like what?" I asked foolishly.

"Like the fact that I still want to spend the rest of my life with you."

"Well, what has changed?"

"I've prayed for a word in due season."

"Well, what did God say?"

"You know," Benji smiled, rubbing my belly like he was sure that we would end up in a blissful situation that wasn't perfect, but was as close to perfect as you could get without being in heaven.

Benji held me close and kissed me as curious onlookers smiled at the little bit of happiness that was sacrificially offered into this day. Nia would be happy for me too. She never did think that Mark was my type, but as usual I had insisted that he was. I demanded to have him and thought that I could make him over into someone that would adore and appreciate me. He was adequate, but he wouldn't have been mine. I had my gift. Benji was here now and he held me as the rain ran down my face, mocking tears. I couldn't help but trust that God was all that mattered and had finally given me the desire of my heart.

I had to believe that I was bigger than my hurts. And when depression tries to take me back to that place where I am unsure of myself, God is there once more to renew my strength. Your beliefs have a way of changing you and taking you to crossroads in your life where you have to make a decision based on the knowledge of His word. Rachel had violated their marriage covenant, she refused to reconcile, and I had my answer.

Chapter Twenty-Five

Sasha and Terry helped me address the wedding invitations. They saved me from having to pay a calligrapher. Pat ordered handmade French lace through her sister Nevi in Paris. Her sister lived near the garment district there and it was easy for her to obtain and export it. Josai and Nicky helped me pick out flowers and a color scheme. We settled on pewter satin dresses from Watters & Watters and silver jewelry to accent the dresses. The flower girls would wear pale yellow dresses and they would all wear pewter colored shoes. Moma thought that pewter was kind of a dismal color for a wedding, but I assured her that compared to the black and white weddings and red and black wedding some people tried to pull off, mine would be classier.

The date was set for four months from today, which didn't seem like a lot of time, but with the help I got from my family and friends, I knew I could do it. September was a wonderful month to get married. Not too hot or humid, and still cool enough to enjoy the last little bit of summer without being too uncomfortable in the dresses. Benji and I had been attending premarital counseling and we vowed to make it work. We were to be equally yoked and had both sought God. His approval alone was enough to give us the confidence to move ahead in our decision to be together. Our pastor would marry us on the 25th day of September. Pastor thought that we could have a potential problem where the spending of money was concerned, so we agreed to pray and seek each other in our spending. Pastor said not to see it as checking in and getting approval or permission from the other to spend the money, but instead to view it as agreeing. I wanted us to agree. Benji felt led to join the church I was attending. They had officially made an announcement of our intent to marry over the pulpit last Sunday.

Moma was excited that we had actually set a date. I had never managed to take the engagement ring off, although I should have. But I couldn't part with the constant reminder of a man who loved me enough to pursue me and seek God for my hand. Rhonda was still warming up to the idea that I was marrying a divorced man. Her relationship with Gene had changed drastically over the course of a couple of months. It had panned out for the better. It had given her something to be happy about. Cheyenne and Benji hit it off finally. They horsed around like brother and sister now. He hardly even remembers that young woman who sat on the windowsill in my apartment lit up like a zombie. Moma and Chey had flown down for a couple of weeks in July. Benji was enjoying the chance to get closer to them. Chey and Benji were acting more like brother and sister than soon to be in-laws. Seems he was not unwilling to forget bad beginnings and first impressions.

After Sunday services, I had been spending most afternoons at Benji's mother's house in Mount Vernon. It was quiet up there and she was genuine and kind. I prayed that she would like me and that we would get along really well. I wanted to be the best daughter-in-law that I could.

She'd cook us an elaborate dinner with homemade biscuits, macaroni and cheese, and whatever else Benji had a taste for, which was usually his favorite, pineapple and honey glazed ham.

"You don't have to go through all this trouble," I'd say.

"You're eating for two, Aaliyah," she would tell me when I'd get concerned about the calories and the fat content. She always put a little extra on my plate.

"I'm fat enough," I kidded. She insisted that I call her Mona, and she was crazy about Nicky, who always showed up with a Modern Bride magazine and pages ripped out with things she thought I'd like. Benji had been living with his mom since Rachel had refused to go to counseling, and had put him and his things out. It didn't matter to him. It confirmed what he already believed; his marriage to Rachel was over. We hadn't officially decided where we would live either, but we knew that wherever we decided to live or relocate to, it wouldn't be a problem, not in the least. We would adjust.

September came. The season of the leaves falling from the trees reminded me of when Benji and I had first started getting serious over a year ago. Mr. Emerson wasn't happy about me and my lack of dedication to the company. I assured him that I was still as dedicated as I always was. I put in my paperwork for maternity leave, and our financial plans and wedding arrangements had fallen into place without a glitch. Benji had inadvertently found out that Rachel had relocated, to an unknown destination. It left Benji feeling angry. He didn't know where the kids were, and he thought it was selfish of her to take such a major step without consulting him. But that was Rachel. Selfish. But he was certain in his heart that it would all be revealed in time. He had faith, and I was so glad that it was faith in God that governed our lives now. He had such a belief and

God that governed our lives now. He had such a belief and at times I didn't know who had more, although it really didn't matter because we were in this together.

Rhonda and Gene would fly into New York a week before the wedding. We hadn't had a sisterly talk in years; I was looking forward to that. She was used to dictating to me what I should do because she was the oldest, and I was always fighting her every step of the way.

"I can't blame you for what Gene did," she said.

"He made his mistakes and I forgave him. I hope Benji makes you happy, Lee."

"He does, Rhonda. He makes me want to sing, girl!"

I was glad that Moma had come to New York. Our relationship had diminished to brief conversations several times a week on the phone, and I relished the chance to get closer to her again. She helped me with the simple things like selecting place settings, which four hours later, wasn't as simple as I had thought. Patterns had to contrast and I could hardly get the reasoning for florals and geometric designs complementing each other. Terry, Josai, Sasha and Nicky all had a hand in planning my bridal shower without me.

"No stripper," I insisted. Nicky giggled hysterically, and I had to remind her that Moma and Mona would be there. Mona handled the caterers and Pat, Cheyenne and Rhonda took the liberty of handling the music, seeking out a photographer and making sure the videographer knew exactly what he was doing when it came to filming weddings. I had finally gotten the opportunity to search around and find a dress that I fell absolutely in love with. Everyone thought that I'd never find a dress in time but I did. God was awesome. I hired a seamstress to use the handmade lace that Pat had her sister import from Paris to design a detachable train for my gown.

219

Benji and I had hardly had a moment's peace or privacy. We made arrangements to go out to dinner after service on Friday; it was our rare time alone together. With all the arrangements and money changing hands, we had little or no time to pray or even sit together and talk. "I miss you, baby," I said looking in his curious brown eyes and thinking he was just as adorable as he was the minute I fell in love with him. I knew I loved him as I watched him from my window, walking down the street after lunch that afternoon we met. He was a confident man, and not at all bothered by the fact that the whole family was planning our entire wedding around us.

I was thankful for a renewed mind and the fact that I no longer let things that people thought influence my decision about anything. I loved things for the sheer enjoyment they gave. I didn't love to seek approval, nor did I have to. I was content to know that I could enjoy reaching my highest potential with a man whom I would allow to do the same.

I had decided that I wasn't going back to work immediately. I might even relocate to San Fernando and work out of that office. I was going to take enough time to be with Benji and the baby. I had decided that the names would be Jada if it was a girl, and Jason if it was a boy. Jada meant "caring" and Jason meant, "healing."

So Jada it was. After nine-and-a-half hours of excruciating labor that was now my initiation into motherhood, a strong feisty baby girl was delivered on August 29th without any complications, and with Benji right by my side. God had delivered me from the valley of darkness and I would offer my child to him in service.

It was a blessing that on occasion, when I would be overheard mentioning that God was good and that I was a Christian, people would want to point out my flaws or want to know what it meant to be saved. Most people used "God," and "Thank you Jesus," as a figure of speech, but it was real for me.

"What are you *saved* from?" they'd ask.

"Hell, death and eternal damnation in the fiery pit," was always my reply. "Saved from the uncertainty and the not knowing." I was proud of the decision I had made to turn over my life to the Creator of it.

Saved didn't mean that I couldn't straighten my hair, or wear jewelry. And being saved didn't mean that I couldn't' enjoy bowling, museums, exotic vacations or make a mistake either. People always came to God with a long checklist of things they wanted to know if they could still do. They had the wrong concept of God. I had the wrong concept too, once. God wasn't limiting, he was liberating! Jesus came to set the captives free, and he who the Son sets free is free indeed!

Terry and I had been spending a lot of time together. She was my support and lifted me up. I realized that those things that we hold on to that bind us and keep us from God are secondary. My relationship with my Savior is not connected to man; my salvation is between God and me. I adhere to His word, keep His commandments and allow Him to be seen through me.

"Girl, isn't God good?" Terry said, after getting accepted into the apprentice program at work.

"God is good like that," I said. "He sure is." I was growing like an oak, not a weed. I knelt nightly and repented of things that I've unknowingly and knowingly done. I wanted to be made over into His complete image. I knew that God wasn't through blessing me yet.

"It's all about Jesus!" "And a deeper relationship with him," Terry added. Yes, my pastor is my teacher and my covering, and we are to be joined to a congregation, but in all things, I take it back to God in prayer. Everything man says must line up with the word of God or else I don't receive it. I've followed man, and listened to their opinions, now I seek the source.

So it was September now, and Jada was almost a month-and-a-half old. She was my joy and my blessing. The weatherman said that there was a slight chance of a thunderstorm all weekend, but I knew God would allow my day to be perfect. It would not rain on my bliss. Besides, I was content with the fact that at least now, Benji and I were on the same page. We had both made mistakes, yet we both appreciated the forgiveness of God. Our struggles, failures and shortcomings didn't define who we were. We are our Father's children, not merely His creation. His children kept his commandments, but it is the faith and the certainty of knowing that He accepts us just as we are, without change being a prerequisite, that makes us love God so much.

Chapter Twenty-Six

I was noticeably decorated with excitement like a child on Christmas morning. A smile had found itself irreplaceably on my face, and Moma was cooking breakfast. The smell of bacon filled the house, reminding me that I hadn't eaten since last night. Nicky, Cheyenne and Rhonda were in the living room, chatting about how they loved the fresh hot buttermilk biscuits Moma used to make.

"Butter, girl, lots of butter," Rhonda said.

"Running off the sides!" Cheyenne added.

"Yeah, and scrapple."

"C'mon y'all. Cut it out. I'm starving," Nicky pleaded. It reminded me of growing up together. There was so much love in our house. Moma would wake everyone and make breakfast on Saturdays and we'd sit around and talk. I was overly-elated about today, but nervous too. So I decided to take a moment to relax and write in my journal as the baby slept. I had been writing a lot lately. I wanted to be able to reflect on my life and be thankful for the chance I had been given to be more than a conqueror.

Josai and Terry arrived simultaneously with their dresses in their protective bags. They were smiling and grinning so that it illuminated my mood and the nervousness subsided a bit. Food was everywhere as the refrigerator now housed the delicate floral bouquets of all the women in the wedding party. Everyone either had pins in their heads or had it masterfully tied up to keep every strand of hair in place. There was music in the house now. Mona was calling to make sure things were coming along without a remote complication.

"I'm not nervous," I assured, shaking my head in attempts to convince both of us.

"I have something special for you, dear. I'll bring it when I come," she said, shooing Benji away from the phone, telling him that he had the rest of his life to talk to me. I adored the idea of the rest of his life.

I was a simple girl. There was nothing I had looked forward to more than my wedding day. I was drifting, thinking of other people in my life I would have liked to share this day with. I could only think of one, Nia. She would have been a bride's maid. I missed her laughter and her confidence in me. She would have loved Jada. Jada was delicate and bright. She was daddy's little girl. She had Benji's eyes.

Nicky was ecstatic. She helped me put on my seamed stockings and helped hook them onto the garter belt.

"How do people wear these things?"

"Lea, are you happy? I mean, are you really happy?" Nicky asked.

"Yes, I've never been happier about anything else in my life."

"I'm glad," Nicky said, hugging me and shedding tears of joy.

"I'll be all right, Nicky."

"I know you will, but I'll miss you."

"I'll always be here for you, Nick."

The phone was ringing and the doorbell was yelling, let me in. Mona arrived looking lovely and elegant in a pale blue crepe wool suit with gold buttons that were stitched with traces of pink. She was wearing a gold locket which held a baby picture of Benjamin.

"Aaliyah, I want you to have this," she said, reaching into her purse, pulling out a navy blue square velvet case that revealed a gold necklace that held three circular diamonds.

"I couldn't, Mona," I shook my head, as she insisted and placed the necklace in my hands and held them.

"Mona, I couldn't take this."

"What do you mean, Lea? It was mine and I want you to have it. I looked like a real bride wearing this, and I want you to do the same," she shared.

"Why you, Lea? Is that what you want to know?"

I nodded.

"I know you'll make Benjamin happy. He's all I have. Promise me you'll make him happy."

"I love him, Mona, he's everything I've prayed for. I will do my best." She kissed me on my forehead and gave me a motherly hug.

Everyone clamored for the mirror, Moma busied herself in the kitchen and I was having difficulty containing what I was experiencing today. I felt very special. The flowergirls sleepily staggered in one by one. There was hair spray and perfume stirring around the apartment.

"Leave this, Moma," I said as she stood in my kitchen washing up the breakfast dishes.

"I'll be fine," she shooed.

"No, you go on Moma, get dressed," I insisted, hugging her and reaching for a strip of bacon.

Rhonda and Cheyenne were laughing about something. They were falling all over each other hysterically.

"Shhh...would you relax," Nicky said. She was on the phone giving James his wake up call.

"I love you too," she said.

"Please get dressed," I said. "I don't want to be late."

"You waited this long," Cheyenne kidded.

Moments later Moma made an entrance with a stunning ivory dress that Rhonda had picked out.

"You go, girl," Nicky said, while Cheyenne and Sasha whistled and everyone else applauded except the sleepyheads. It had a gold buglebead neckline and Moma's hair held slight curls that were accented by matte gold circular clip-on earrings.

Everyone looked beautiful, like right out of the pages of 'Modern Bride.' Nails were done and hair looked fabulous.

"I can't believe this is actually happening," I whispered to Josai.

"He loves you, you love him, enjoy it girl!"

"Trust me I will enjoy every moment of it."

"That's right, Lea, the past is over, this is now."

And I realized I couldn't have put it better myself.

Chapter Twenty-Seven

There had to be about twenty-four dozen yellow tulips draped lovingly over the altar in the church. The flowers were fragrant and the whole church had the freshly scented aroma of nature's perfume. Baby's breaths and miniature white roses were intertwined and strung along the pews giving the effect of lace. Most of the guests had arrived and there was a certainty in the air. The sweetness of the flowers nectar gave promise to a day that had longed to be fulfilled in my heart. There were many changes that my life had gone through, but I cherished this moment and the silence that God had afforded me to hear his still voice and bring me to this point.

I stood in the foyer waiting to enter the church, and through my veil I could see all the heads were turned in my direction. I was wearing a richly textured satin dress that had pearls woven into the lace and a row of buttons up the back. The bridesmaids fluffed my dress, smoothed out my detachable lace train and fidgeted with anything else that needed sprucing. Moma and Mona fussed with my hair and placed strands where they thought they belonged as I focused on the event that would change my last name and my life.

The church was filled with familiar faces, some that grinned and others whose mouths were contorted and quivering as tears welled in their eyes. Pat waved discreetly as if not to distract. My hands were full as I stood lifting my dress, while Terry double-checked my stockings to make sure the white seams up the back were straight.

Pat, Justin, his girlfriend, and Sean sat with the newest addition to their family. A healthy baby girl with a head full of colorful ribbons. She had tipped the scale at barely under ten pounds. They all seemed content with each other, and the tension that had preceded the pregnancy had diminished considerably. Justin was sixteen now and almost a man. A fact that Pat could no longer deny.

Todd and Lisa had made it all the way to New York with the kids. It seemed that they were back together again. They didn't seem to know what they wanted to do, but then today was my day. I would not worry or frown.

I thought of how I would cautiously make my way down the aisle, and I replayed this whole event over and over again in my head, banishing doubt to a place that was far removed from my mind. I allowed myself to think that as reserved as they appeared to be, the bridesmaids would all tumble in an uncoordinated frenzy, making barbaric attempts to catch my bouquet as I tossed it. This running after the bouquet was merely a superstitious representation of who would be the next to marry. So, I prayed in my mind, "Lord bless them all, keep the ones who are married in tune with their spouse and their spouses' needs, and keep their spouses in tune with them. And, Lord, bless the lives of the ones who are single, bring them someone that you have handpicked, Lord, so that they are equally yoked. Show them that you can do all things, Father."

My pastor stood in front of the congregation, assuming his role as the head and the covering. He adjusted his robe and opened up his Bible to what I guessed was the verse that Benji and I had handpicked for our ceremony, Matthew 18:19. The pews were polished to a high shine, and the multi-hued stained glass windows that formed colorful outlines of a cross, each reflected sparkling beauty that made my day all the more special.

Benji stood impatiently tugging at his cuffs and clasped his hands in front of him as if each hand was comforting the other. He nodded his head to reassure me and I nodded back and smiled. He had been considering cutting his locks off but had opted to trim them instead. I loved his hair. He was clean-shaven and handsome, to say the least. He was also self-assured and goal-oriented. Those were qualities I've always found irresistible, but then God knew the desires of my heart before I had even asked. Benji elbowed his cousin who was his best man. He mumbled something and his cousin quickly patted his left upper pocket checking for the ring with beads of perspiration forming on his brow.

Soft instrumentals were playing as I had forgone the traditional "Here Comes the Bride."

"There was more to life than hoping to get married," I thought out loud. There was God. I looked around earnestly as this day stepped right off of the pages of a romance novel and offered me the starring role. How could I explain to anyone why I was so happy? Not only was I in love, but I had been, for the most part, obedient.

The flower girls were children that were borrowed from friends and distant family members. They were adorned in simple pale yellow velvet dresses, and made their way into the assembly, decorating the aisle to and fro with silver confetti, as the thought of crushed rose petals wasn't very appealing. There were light whispers fluttering around as the bridesmaids began entering the church each coupled with an usher. Flashbulbs went off as the photographers began capturing the moment that I would come to remember as the happiest day of my life.

Josai looked radiant in her pewter chiffon dress and her hair back in a simple bun accented with tiny pearls. She was all smiles and bubbled over with laughter.

"Shhhh," I said, as she reminded me, "I told you, I told you. You found someone." I couldn't help but smile. Nicky walked down the aisle with James. I imagined that she might be rehearsing in her mind how her wedding would be. She was graceful and almost bride-like.

Cheyenne was more than overjoyed to be a part of the wedding. I remember she couldn't wait for me to return from Aruba to begin planning it. There hadn't been a wedding in the immediate family for almost ten years. That was when Rhonda and Gene had tied the knot in '86. Chey had truly come a long way. She said she had tossed the idea around about returning to New York for good.

"I miss it," she said. She just wasn't sure if Moma would be willing to part with all that Florida sunshine though.

Terry was calm and subdued as she gave my gown one last fluff. "You know you deserve this, Aaliyah."

"I know," I smiled, not sure if I was as convinced as I sounded. She hugged me as we said a silent prayer, thanking God for allowing everything to go off without a hitch.

"To God be the glory," she said. "Amen!"

Sasha smiled, teary-eyed. She hugged and kissed my cheek, not fully understanding what change had prompted me to forgive her. She looked so innocent and her eyes were bright with excitement as she held her bouquet of pale yellow roses that glistened with the drops of water that kept them alive overnight.

"I love you, Lea."

"I know you do, girl."

"I'm so sorry," she began.

"Sasha, everything happens for a reason. I know that now."

"Are you happy, Lea?"

"I'm ecstatic," I nodded frantically. Mark escorted Sasha into the church and he seemed nervous looking back at me, but I was convinced that this was my day. The day I had waited a lifetime for. The day that God knew would happen. Even when Mark didn't show that night, God knew. This was the day that was predestined before the foundations of the world, I thought, as I took my first steps into holy matrimony. Forgiven.

What God Expects of Men and Women in Marriage

Trust is essential. Partners must foster and possess a constant belief and a reliant expectation in each other.

Faithfulness and being true to one's word, one's vows and adhering to the Biblical principles of marriage is vital.

Affection and emotional fondness for your spouse yields a loving relationship where both partners convey their devotion continuously.

Communicating and sharing with each other your true thoughts and opinions openly and honestly, makes marriages last.

Supporting each other's ideas, thoughts and feelings (even in prayer) helps sustain the marital commitment.

Complying and cooperating readily with each other in accordance with the Word, pleases not only your spouse, but God.

Intimacy is a special private part of marriage. Sexual familiarity, and a constant personal closeness, leaves little or no room for intrusion.

Submitting to each other's feelings and needs is not a power trip or a weakness, there is beauty in submission.

Being appealing affects more than just the eyes. We must purposely attract, amuse and stimulate our partner's mind and emotions daily.

Awareness is the key! Be aware of the enemy's devices. If we fail in any of the above attributes, it can be the beginning of the end. Make and keep it a joint effort to attain your lifelong goals together.

AMEN

Sometimes I Cry $12.95

Order Form

Milligan Books
1425 West Manchester, Suite B,
Los Angeles, California 90047
(323) 750-3592

Mail Check or Money Order to:
Milligan Books

Name _____ Date _____

Address _____

City_____ State _____ Zip Code_____

Day telephone _____

Evening telephone_____

Book title _____

Number of books ordered ___ Total cost .... $_____

Sales Taxes (CA Add 8.25%) .... $_____

Shipping & Handling $3.00 per book .... $_____

Total Amount Due..$_____

· Check   · Money Order   Other Cards _____

· Visa   · Master Card   Expiration Date _____

Credit Card No. _____

Driver's License No. _____

Signature   Date